CONTROVERSIES IN SOVIET SOCIAL THOUGHT

I0689534

CONTROVERSIES IN SOVIET SOCIAL THOUGHT

DEMOCRATIZATION, SOCIAL JUSTICE, AND THE EROSIÓN OF OFFICIAL IDEOLOGY

Murray Yanowitch

LONDON AND NEW YORK

First published 1991 by M.E. Sharpe

Published 2015 by Routledge
2 Park Square, Milton Park, Abingdon, Oxon OX14 4RN
711 Third Avenue, New York, NY 10017, USA

Routledge is an imprint of the Taylor & Francis Group, an informa business

Library of Congress Cataloging-in-Publication Data

Yanowitch, Murray
Controversies in Soviet social thought :
democratization, social justice, and the erosion of official ideology
/ by Murray Yanowitch.
p.   cm.
Includes bibliographical references and index.
ISBN 0-87332-558-3. — ISBN 0-87332-881-7 (pbk.)
1. Soviet Union—Social policy.
2. Soviet Union—Politics and government—1985–   .
3. Perestroika.
4. Soviet Union—Social conditions—1970–   .
I. Title.
HN527.Y36   1991
361.6′1′0947—dc20
91-14600
CIP

ISBN 13: 9780873328814 (pbk)
ISBN 13: 9780873325585 (hbk)

CONTENTS

PREFACE

The chapters that follow document the substantial expansion of intellectual freedom that characterized the first five years of Mikhail Gorbachev's political leadership in the Soviet Union. In these essays we examine the discussions and controversies that emerged during this period on a variety of issues associated with the process of democratization (first in the workplace, and then in the political sphere), the theme of distributive justice, and the erosion of Marxist-Leninist ideology.

Our review of these discussions makes it clear that the diversity and richness of Soviet views on these matters cannot be readily encapsulated within the familiar but simplistic distinction between "democrats" and "hard-liners." Moreover, it is not only the diversity of views that is of interest here but also the "escalating" quality of some of the discussions—the readiness to move beyond what previously might have appeared to be a relatively bold position, so that ultimately the most "sacred" truths become open to question.

Given the rapidity of change in the Soviet Union, it is almost obligatory to acknowledge that some of the discussions reviewed here have been superseded or overtaken by events. But their significance is surely not diminished by this fact, which itself illustrates what might be called the "expansionary logic" of the reform discussion. For example, in chapter 2 we consider conflicting Soviet responses to the issue of democratization of workplace management. Some of the principal discussions reviewed here naturally focus on the issue of managerial elections and the appropriate functions of elected work councils, as provided under legislation that was in effect in 1988–89. More recent legislation has essentially eliminated such elections (at least for higher-level managerial positions in state enterprises) and significantly reduced the role of work councils. But these changes hardly diminish the importance of some of our principal findings in chapter 2—for example, that Soviet discussions of workplace democratization provided a forum for the propagation of democratic values, and that multicandidate elections (although by no means common practice) were explicitly defended and popularized in the context of the enterprise before they became "normal" procedure in the selection of deputies to the new parliament and local soviets in 1989–90.

How much scope can there be for intellectual freedom—freedom of expression—in a society that has barely begun the transition to a market economy and in which productive resources remain overwhelmingly under state ownership, at least in a legal or formal sense? We do not pose this question in order to suggest that the essays that follow can provide anything approximating a definitive answer to it, but they certainly have some bearing on any serious attempt to confront this question. Our point can be made quite simply. Chapter 1 provides some examples of reformist themes and democratic sentiments in the social-science literature in the immediate pre-Gorbachev period. While they illustrate some basic continuities in critical social thought over the whole decade of the 1980s, most of these earlier discussions have a distinctly muted and restrained quality compared with those that emerged shortly thereafter. The Soviet literature examined in chapters 2–5 appeared mainly in 1987–89. By comparison with anything that appeared earlier in the decade (or in the preceding sixty years), the discussions and controversies reviewed in these chapters marked the emergence of a significant degree of intellectual freedom in the Soviet Union. But it would be difficult, if not impossible, to demonstrate that the expanding limits of freedom of expression in 1987–89 were preceded or accompanied by significant movement toward a "free market"—as the term is normally understood—or toward the privatization of productive property. Important changes in this direction followed rather than preceded the freeing of intellectual life. Thus our provisional, if not very illuminating, response to the question posed at the beginning of this paragraph is: "considerable," judging by the brief Soviet experience of the late 1980s.

Readers will undoubtedly decide for themselves whether the evidence of intellectual ferment presented in chapters 2–5 justifies our characterization of the late 1980s as a period of substantial freedom of expression in the Soviet Union. Our review of Soviet discussions of the linkage between Marxism and Stalinism and the examples of Soviet social-democratic and neoconservative literature examined in chapter 5 probably represent the strongest justification for such a characterization. We would also suggest that the popularization of concepts such as "civil society" and "political pluralism," the positive reassessment of "bourgeois democracy" (chapter 3), and some rather novel arguments in defense of economic inequality (chapter 4) provide additional evidence of the expanding boundaries of intellectual freedom in the Soviet Union during this period. Perhaps of greatest significance in these discussions are the occasional signs of the gradual development of the rare habit of civilized controversy on current political and social issues. This process has a long way to go, and one can only hope that it will not be reversed.

The author is most grateful to Patricia Kolb, executive editor at M.E. Sharpe, for frequent discussions on the substance of these essays and for seeing the project through to completion.

CONTROVERSIES IN SOVIET SOCIAL THOUGHT

1

Reformist Undercurrents in the Pre-Gorbachev Period

It is now clear that the immediate pre-Gorbachev years were more than merely years of "stagnation." This was also a period in which the unfolding of debate on economic reform helped set the stage for the reforms introduced by the Gorbachev political leadership in the late 1980s (Hewett, 1988, ch. 6; Åslund, 1989, ch. 5). But the reformist themes sounded in the first half of the decade were not confined to the strictly economic literature. They also appeared in the writings of some of the country's leading sociologists and psychologists. Indeed, our principal concern here is to demonstrate that the multidisciplinary reformist undercurrents of the years of "stagnation" provided a language, a set of ideas, and a conceptual apparatus on which a future political leadership would draw and also contributed to the intellectual discourse and controversies of the Gorbachev years examined in subsequent chapters. To put it in somewhat different but perhaps more direct terms, the break with the past represented by the Gorbachev years also rests on certain continuities.

Since the discussions among economists in the early 1980s (including the writings of the economic sociologist T.I. Zaslavskaia) have already been examined in the Western literature, we focus here mainly on some other significant, but less familiar, illustrations of reformist undercurrents in the immediate pre-Gorbachev period.

On "Social Innovations"

The early 1980s saw the appearance of several volumes on what was essentially a new theme in the Soviet social-science literature—the sociology of innovation processes (Lapin, 1980, 1981, 1982). The volumes consisted largely of papers delivered at conferences held under the aegis of the Academy of Sciences Institute of Systems Research and a subdivision of the Soviet Sociological Association concerned with the sociology of organizations. Given the novelty of the subject and the nature of the sponsoring institutions, it is hardly surprising that among the principal objectives of these publications was "the elaboration of a common language to describe innovation processes." The relevance of this literature to our concern with reformist undercurrents becomes apparent when we consider some of the typologies of innovations formulated here and the particular categories singled out for special attention.

The basic typology of innovations introduced in the earliest of the above volumes, and repeated and elaborated in the later ones, involved a classification according to the "objective content" of the innovation: (a) new products, (b) new technology, (c) social innovations, or "new organizational structures of management," and (d) composite innovations (some combination of the preceding three types). There appears to be nothing striking about such a commonsense classification, but it was typically accompanied by the observation that such a classification represented a broader approach than was usual in the past, when the "problematic" of innovations was virtually identified with new technology. For some participants in these discussions the point that needed stressing was that the importance of organizational innovations had received inadequate attention relative to the role of new technology (Lapin, 1980, pp. 5, 26; 1981, p. 6; 1982, p. 38). Perhaps the most persistent voice in the early 1980s appealing for recognition of the general principle that "organizational innovations are needed today no less than technological innovations" was that of the sociologist A.I. Prigozhin (1983, pp. 6, 14, 162).

Another distinction introduced in these early discussions was based on "the degree of novelty" of innovations. The principal distinction here was between "radical" and "modifying" innovations. In the very general terminology commonly used in this literature, the former implied "fundamentally new" means of satisfying needs and the introduction of "qualitative changes" in human activity. Modifying innovations referred essentially to those that involved an "improvement" in existing mechanisms, whether technical or social. But the significant point here is that as early as 1980 the literature on innovations pointed to the relatively low share of radical innovations as a factor reducing "the effectiveness of innovation processes" and as making for the "inadequate dynamism" of the economy (Lapin, 1980, pp. 7, 12). By early 1984, recognition of the need for radical innovations was no longer confined to esoteric papers delivered at conferences of the Institute of Systems Research but had moved on to the more accessible pages of the party's principal monthly organ, *Kommunist* (Prigozhin, 1984). Moreover, the author of the *Kommunist* article, which stressed that basic or radical innovations were now (1984) "most in need of experimentation," was among those who had begun to invoke the new language of radical innovations in publications issued in 1980–82.

What particular types of social or organizational or managerial innovations (these terms were typically used synonymously) did this variety of pre-Gorbachev reformist thought recommend? Although the details of a reformist program are not to be found in this literature, there was no mystery about the general direction of the proposed innovations. A report summarizing the proceedings of a conference on managerial innovations noted that a principal theme was that the "most promising" innovations were those that increased the independence of economic organizations (Zhezhko, 1982). The frequent reiteration in Prigozhin's writings of the need for "self-regulation" and "self-organization" in the normal functioning of enterprises clearly pointed in the same direction (1983, pp. 61–73). Lapin and Prigozhin (1982) reported on some important ideas introduced at a conference on "social innovations" conducted under the auspices of the Tavistock Institute in England. Among the most interesting workshops at the conference were those in which participants focused on opportunities "to overcome role boundaries" and change "power relations" within organizations. In the same spirit, but in somewhat more precise language, Prigozhin shortly afterward (1983, p. 99)—and in a somewhat more accessible publication—formulated a principle that he suggested was generally accepted in sociology: The larger the proportion of "middle-level" and "lower-level" personnel among those making decisions in organizations, the "more efficient" the organization is likely to be.

It is hardly surprising that in the months immediately following Gorbachev's accession to power, the language that had emerged earlier in the literature on organizational innovations was to be heard again, but this time in somewhat "escalated" form. Thus for Lapin and Sazonov a critical issue had become that of raising the "receptivity" of organizational structures to "permanent radical innovations" (1985, p. 70). Relying on somewhat more direct language, Prigozhin argued that the time had come for "the serious restructuring" of economic management "as a whole," rather than partial changes in the existing system (1985, pp. 38–39). But the continuities in reformist thought that concern us here were not confined to the writings of a couple of sociologists attached to the Institute of Systems Research. Other illustrations are considered below.

"Democratization" and the New Technology

Some of the sociological literature of the early 1980s (and the months immediately following the Gorbachev accession) sought to link the need for reformist policies with the emergence of a new technology and associated changes in the composition of the work force. The writings of L.A. Gordon and A.K. Nazimova (1983, 1984, 1985), particularly their stress on the urgency of democratization in the workplace and in the society at large, illustrate this brand of reformist thought. The logic of their argument can be readily understood if we briefly consider their typology of prevailing "technological types of production." These include (a) early industrial (or preindustrial), (b) developed industrial, and (c) scientific-industrial. Each of these technological types corresponds to a particular occupational mix and leaves its imprint on the behavior patterns of those included in its orbit.

The first of these applies to sectors that employ mainly manual labor supplemented by relatively simple instruments, but work here is not "organically included in machine production" (1985, p. 95; also 1984, p. 24). A significant proportion of agricultural labor, construction work, longshore operations, and packing and cleaning jobs fall into this early industrial (or preindustrial) category. A minimum of formal schooling is required for adequate job performance. For Gordon and Nazimova this type of technology and the jobs associated with it represent "a sort of enclave of times past, of social labor's bygone days" (1983b, p. 70).

As for the second technological type (developed industrial), work here is an "organic part of a machine production process" that is most clearly represented by the conveyor belt or assembly-line technology. While most of the jobs generated by this type of technology involve mechanized labor, such labor retains "primarily a physical character," with workers often functioning as appendages of machines (Gordon and Nazimova, 1985, pp. 96–98, 104). The "machine system" governs the rhythm of work and the sequence of operations, leaving little scope for worker discretion and "self-organization." Such technology appears to require, or at least to promote, "strictly directive" forms of management. Put somewhat differently, it encourages an "overassessment of centralism and an underassessment of the democratic principle" in public life (Gordon and Nazimova, 1984, pp. 26–27). Approximately seven or eight years of general education, sometimes supplemented by brief vocational training, is usually sufficient to meet typical job requirements.

But it is the third technological type (scientific-industrial) that is decisive for the future of the Soviet economy and society. Writing in the early 1980s, Gordon and Nazimova estimated that such technology accounted for less than a fifth of the nonagricultural work force. But these writers linked their case for systemic reforms to the projected increase in the relative importance of such technology. The Soviet system's ability to assimilate the new technology urgently required far-reaching institutional changes. "The emergence of scientific-industrial production is one of the factors that makes the development of democracy in our country particularly urgent at present" (Gordon and Nazimova, 1983b, p. 71). How did they justify this position?

This Soviet category of scientific-industrial production characterizes the kind of work that some of the Western literature associates with "postindustrial" or cybernetic technology (Hirschhorn, 1986). Where such technology dominates the production process, a large proportion of the work force is employed in the storage, processing, and transmission of information. "Scientific services" become an increasingly important sector of the economy. Workers are increasingly engaged in directly servicing fully automated production processes, or processes guided with the help of "automatic manipulators and industrial robots." Occupations such as programmers and operators of electronic computers, laboratory workers, and quality-control personnel become increasingly important. Workers' jobs become intellectually more demanding, and traditional distinctions between the job content of workers and "specialists" begin to break down. Adequate job performance requires at the very least a complete general secondary education (ten years of schooling) often followed by specialized vocational training.

Perhaps most important in distinguishing work in scientific-industrial production from its predecessor is that such work "is not subordinate to a strict algorithm." Workers must be ready to confront "nonstandard operations," to solve tasks "created by unexpected situations" (or "under conditions of uncertainty"). The production process under such circumstances requires workers with a capacity for "self-organization," the habit of exercising initiative and taking independent decisions. These are the characteristics of the work process under the new technology that, in the view of Gordon and Nazimova, make "active and constant worker participation in management" a matter of "direct production necessity" (1984, pp. 27–29; 1985, pp. 108–13). But such participation can only become a reality, they insist, if enterprise autonomy is substantially increased and the "directive-administrative" methods of planning and management rooted in the forced industrialization of the 1930s are abandoned.

Gordon and Nazimova were not alone in making a serious case for the democratization of management (Yanowitch, 1989, pp. viii–ix). But the concepts and language that appeared in their writings of 1983–85 (the need for restructuring [*perestroika*] of the economic mechanism and of all spheres of public life, for "radical" improvements in relations of production, for strengthening democratic principles in the management of production and in the life of society) anticipated to a remarkable degree what was to become the essential core of reformist discourse in the late 1980s.

The Theme of "Social Justice"

One of the principal rallying cries in the discussions and controversies of the late 1980s was the need to implement "social justice." This matter is considered in some detail in chapter 4. But like other controversies of this period, this one also elaborated and responded to ideas that had been voiced in the reformist writings of the early 1980s. How was the concept of "social justice" used in the literature of the immediate pre-Gorbachev period, and what demands were made in its name?

Perhaps the principal voice in the literature on social justice in the first half of the 1980s was that of sociologist V.Z. Rogovin. For Rogovin the concept of social justice had its most obvious applications in the sphere of "distributive relations." But he also recognized that even within this area the concept had come to be used in a steadily expanding context. Thus, while in the past the demand for social justice had been largely associated with the need to "liquidate poverty," in more recent years it had become increasingly linked with "the idea of social equality in the broadest sense of the word," including equality not only in economic status but also in access to education and to "the adoption of socially significant decisions" (Akademiia nauk, 1982, pp. 10–11). While Rogovin made it clear that he was referring here to the way that the concept of social justice had come to be used by "mass movements" throughout the world, there was nothing to suggest that he regarded the broader meaning recently attached to the concept as inappropriate to Soviet circumstances. The bulk of his own writings on this theme, however, focus on "distributive relations" in the more conventional sense of inequalities in the distribution of real income.

Rogovin recognized that there was a "certain contradiction" between the two basic functions of Soviet distributive policy. The first of these functions involved ensuring "the maximum possible convergence in living standards" of the country's various social groups, given the current stage of economic development. The second function required the implementation of the familiar socialist principle of distribution, namely, wage differentiation in accordance with the differing labor contribution of workers, or a "strict commensurability between what a person gives to society and what he receives from society" (ibid., pp. 12–14). Obviously, the application of this principle always limited the extent to which society could move toward greater socioeconomic equality. But the attainment of the "maximum possible" degree of such equality (the first of the two principal elements of a socialist distribution policy) similarly imposed limits on the extent of income differentiation rooted in differences in work performed. Reliance on both principles was necessary to ensure that distributive policy would be guided by "social criteria" as well as strictly "economic criteria." Accepting the need for an "optimal combination" of these principles, Rogovin directed most of his criticism at what he regarded as "socially unjustified" inequalities in income distribution.

The reformist nature of Rogovin's discussion of distributive justice becomes apparent when he turns to the issue of providing all youngsters with "approximately equal opportunities" to reveal and develop their abilities. "If some children—because of the activity of their parents—have opportunities that others of the same age do not have, such a situation cannot be regarded as just" (ibid., p. 13). Hence the need for policies directed at equalizing the "starting positions" of youngsters through the distribution of such vital goods and services as medical care, preschool facilities, housing space, vacation facilities, opportunities for skill acquisition, and so on, without charge or at subsidized prices out of "social consumption funds." But in fact there was abundant evidence, which Rogovin presented (ibid., pp. 12–14; Akademiia nauk, 1984, pp. 96–113), demonstrating that higher-paid social groups often had greater access to such free and subsidized facilities than low-income groups. Recent studies had shown, for example, that high-income families were almost twice as likely to make use of preschool child-care facilities as low-income families (91.6 percent versus 48.2 percent), and that the former group was also more likely than the latter to send its children to Pioneer camps, to live in separate apartments, and to have access to superior medical facilities. Not only did such practices seem incompatible with the provision of equal opportunities for children's development but, more generally, they conflicted with the designated function of "social consumption funds," namely, the (free or subsidized) distribution of basic services in a manner that would reduce the inequalities in real income associated with distribution in accordance with work performed.

To meet this situation Rogovin called for the implementation of the principle of "equal access to free and reduced-price (*l'gotnye*) vital goods" (Akademiia nauk, 1984, p. 102). More specifically, the proposal involved the establishment of a "socially guaranteed minimum" of basic goods and services (housing space, medical care, child-care facilities, etc.) that would be "equal for all" and would be provided without charge or at nominal prices. Acquisition of such items in excess of the "social norm" (the guaranteed minimum) would be perfectly legal but would require the payment of normal market prices. Thus it was not so much the very idea of unequal distribution of such facilities that was the target of Rogovin's criticism as the privileged access of higher-paid groups to their free (or almost free) distribution. Perhaps anticipating attacks from critics constantly on the lookout for signs of "egalitarianism," Rogovin made it clear that he fully supported measures to "liquidate socially unjustified leveling tendencies in the payment of labor" (1982, p. 8). But he seemed obviously more concerned with identifying socially unjustified inequalities, the kind engendered when ministries and departments—which are assigned highly unequal priorities (and therefore resources)—were relied upon to provide vital services to their "own" workers.

The issue of distributive justice was invoked in a similar spirit by other writers during these years. Thus A.N. Shokhin was explicitly critical of the kind of unequal access to consumer goods represented by "special systems of sale of goods and provision of services" designed to serve restricted groups of eligible purchasers (Akademiia nauk, 1984, p. 153). It did not require much reading between the lines to recognize this as directed against special distribution channels available to privileged groups of state and party officials. N.I. Alekseev linked the implementation of social justice at the workplace with the need to develop "democratic principles" in the selection and promotion of cadres and in the management of production (Akademiia nauk, 1982, pp. 135, 138–39). While this was not the typical context in which social justice was invoked in Soviet discussions, it was clearly in accord with Rogovin's association of this concept with social equality in "the broadest sense," including access to "the adoption of socially significant decisions."

The months immediately following Gorbachev's assumption of political leadership saw an "escalation" in the literature directed against income and wealth inequalities that appeared to conflict with accepted norms of distributive justice (Markov, 1985; Rogovin, 1985a). But this marked the beginning of a debate to which we shall return later. Our objective here has been to identify a component of pre-Gorbachev reformist thought that served as a background to this debate.

Social Psychology and Socially Desirable Values

The "academic" as well as "popular" writings of some of the country's leading psychologists in 1983–84 encouraged the development of the kinds of values and attitudes that later in the decade would seem to represent the very embodiment (in a psychological sense) of the Gorbachev reforms. We refer, in particular, to the writings of K. Muzdybaev and I. Kon.

Muzdybaev's studies focused on factors promoting and obstructing the development of a sense of personal responsibility, the "psychology of responsibility" (1983). Stated in the most general and simple terms, a principal theme of Muzdybaev's work was that the opportunity for a choice among alternatives, for exercising a "conscious preference" for a particular type of behavior, was a necessary condition for responsibility. Put somewhat differently, the greater the opportunity for "self-determination," the greater the awareness of and fulfillment of one's role obligations (Muzdybaev, 1983, pp. 21–22). But given the increasingly serious problems of indifferent work performance and poor work discipline in the late 1970s and early 1980s,[1] it is hardly surprising that Muzdybaev focused particular attention on behavior at the workplace. The general question posed by Muzdybaev was the following: How do differences in forms of work organization affect workers' sense of responsibility and job performance? More specifically, what was the impact on worker responsibility of—among other factors—(a) the presence or absence of "an independent work section," (b) differences in the degree of worker independence in choosing the method of implementing a job assignment, (c) the presence or absence of opportunities for workers independently to record the results of their labor, and (d) differences in the frequency of supervision of job performance by foremen?

Muzdybaev's findings, based on a study of the work behavior

of a sample of 540 Leningrad workers as well as a review of the relevant foreign literature, appeared quite clear-cut: increased independence in the work process and increased scope for "self-determination," typically operated to heighten a worker's sense of responsibility and to improve work performance (ibid., pp. 183–88). Muzdybaev was particularly intrigued by the impact of variations in the frequency of supervision. "One would think that the more frequent the supervision [*kontrol'*], the more diligently would production duties be fulfilled. The data obtained ... do not confirm this. The level of responsibility was lower among those whose work performance was checked more frequently" (ibid., p. 187).

The implications of his findings seemed unambiguous for Muzdybaev. The kind of work organization that would give workers "maximum independence" (in relation to the job characteristics cited above)[2] could be expected to make them more responsible and to improve their fulfillment of their job obligations. Why should this be the case? The possibility of exercising independence in the work process, of making one's own decisions, heightens an individual's sense of importance and self-respect. Workers who "feel that they themselves control the situation are more often satisfied with their work, are more actively involved in the labor process, and their productivity reaches a high level." The absence of opportunities for such decision making promotes "alienation from work" (ibid., p. 188).

Muzdybaev's writings may be regarded as part of the "academic" literature on this subject and thus were unlikely to have had many readers. But their message must have reached a considerable audience in 1984 when I. Kon reviewed Muzdybaev's work in *Novyi mir* (1984b). That message, in Kon's formulation, was that the worker's sense of personal responsibility was "proportional" to his participation in decision making at the workplace. Nor was the relevance of this message confined to the workplace alone. In another publication reaching an even wider audience, *Pravda*, Kon appealed for the encouragement of independence and the capacity for genuine participation in decision making in children's early schooling and family upbringing

(1984a). Indeed, Kon's writings in the immediate pre-Gorbachev period may be regarded as a sustained appeal for a psychological *perestroika* in the spirit of democratic values and independence in thought and action. A particularly clear illustration of these sentiments is apparent in Kon's discussion of the concept of conformity.

Describing, in somewhat idealized terms, the kind of individual required in a rapidly changing modern society with its constantly increasing flow of information, Kon sketched the following picture (1984c, p. 153): "His thinking must be open and turned to the world . . . and at the same time it must not be conformist, under the control of others, for the leveling of human individuality inevitably transforms society into an anthill." The conformist, for Kon, is typically an individual who seeks to shift responsibility for his behavior to others. In the Soviet context conformity is rooted in the conception of "the collective as some kind of external force to which the individual must passively submit."[3] Kon notes that the implicit justification for conformist behavior is reflected in the following common expressions. "The collective cannot be wrong." "The individual who comes out against the collective is an egoist." But Kon explicitly rejects the notion of the infallibility of the collective. The conformist is "always with the collective" essentially because it is more peaceful that way. There is "no need to struggle or to think." For Kon this kind of peace represents a betrayal of both the collective and oneself (ibid., p. 285).

In this situation the most urgent "social-pedagogical task" is that of cultivating independence in people, of creating the conditions necessary for the "free exchange of opinions, the direct and open discussion of all urgent issues." Not only is there no reason to fear a diversity of views, insists Kon, but such diversity should be welcomed, for it is a necessary condition for reaching the appropriate decision on any particular issue. Hence his appeal for judging collectives not only in terms of such criteria as group solidarity and proper "ideological foundations" but by the degree to which they provided a democratic atmosphere (*demokratichnost'*) that permitted the "unhindered consideration of new ideas (ibid., pp. 280, 286).

There is no ambiguity in Kon's view of the institutional structures that would encourage the transformation of unthinking conformity into a sense of personal responsibility. "The more democratic the mechanism of management and the broader the group of people actively participating in it, the deeper their sense of responsibility" (ibid., pp. 306–7). In light of all this, it seems perfectly natural that there should have been a basic continuity between Kon's earlier writings and those published in the months immediately following Gorbachev's accession to political leadership. Thus an article by Kon that appeared in July 1985 opens with the declaration that there can hardly be "a more valuable personal quality than independence" (1985, p. 42). Here again is an intellectual whose ideas on these and related issues in the first half of the 1980s would be widely echoed in the years that followed.[4]

If there is a single theme that recurs in all of these early reformist undercurrents, it is the need for democratization in the sense of enhanced opportunities for popular participation in decision making on public issues. But in each case the need for such participation is justified in somewhat different terms. For Prigozhin and Lapin "organizational efficiency" required greater participation by lower- and middle-level personnel. For Gordon and Nazimova the new "scientific-industrial" technology could not realize its potential without the extension of workplace democratization. Some of the literature on distributive justice, although mainly concerned with other issues, linked democratization with social equality in "the broadest sense." And as we have just seen, for Muzdybaev and Kon there was a critical link between more participatory "management structures" and the acceptance of responsibility. What is most striking about all of these writings is that if they had first appeared in the late 1980s (instead of during the earlier years of "stagnation"), they would almost certainly have been regarded as part of the "literature of *perestroika*."

Notes

1. There is abundant evidence of this in the Soviet literature. For one example, see Zaslavskaia and Kupriianova (1987), p. 27.

2. Muzdybaev also sought to determine the influence on workers' sense of responsibility of brigade versus individual work (the evidence did not clearly point in favor of one or the other) and of jobs involving the assembly of a "finished product" versus "detail work" (the former heightened workers' awareness of their responsibility).

3. It should be noted, however, that Kon distinguished between conformity as the habitual submission to group pressure and the process of "collective self-determination" in which the individual "consciously" accepts the basic values of the group and is prepared to defend them, even in the face of the hostile majority outside the group (1984c, p. 279).

4. Although we have based our discussion here on Kon's writings issued in 1984, he expressed essentially similar views in 1980 (*Literaturnaia gazeta*, no. 52) and quite possibly earlier.

2

Toward "Democratization" of the Workplace

We have seen that worker participation in management in the Soviet Union is not something that emerged as a public issue only during the Gorbachev period. It was the subject of serious public discourse in the economic, sociological, and legal literature beginning with the efforts at economic reform of the 1960s and continuing through the immediate pre-Gorbachev years (Moses, 1987; Yanowitch, 1978, 1985). But there can be no doubt that since 1985 Soviet discussions of this theme have been immeasurably richer and more far-reaching than in earlier years, and statutory changes governing labor-management relations contain at least the potential for significant changes in the distribution of authority at the workplace. Whether these discussions and statutory changes presage the implementation of something that deserves to be called "production democracy" (a goal invoked with increasing frequency in the Soviet literature in the late 1980s) remains to be determined, but it is already clear that Soviet managerial ideology has been profoundly transformed. How can we characterize the new managerial ideology, and, in particular, how has the Soviet literature in this area sought to reconcile the "democratization" of management with the need for "professionalism" in management? What are some of the principal justifications offered for the "democratization" of management? These are among the main issues that concern us in this chapter.

The importance of these issues is rooted in their close connection to ongoing efforts to implement "radical," decentralizing, market-oriented economic reforms. Worker participation in management is also one aspect of a new, broader theme that has begun to be discussed seriously—the general "democratization" of Soviet society. Hence it should come as no surprise that discussions of workplace democratization have become an arena of controversy between reformist and "conservative" forces. But it would be an oversimplification to regard the diversity of views on this issue as reflecting merely the conflicting positions of supporters and opponents of democratization. Our examination of the variety of views expressed in the literature should make this clear.

The new ideology of management, the controversies surrounding it, and the participatory mechanisms embodied in new legal statutes—all of which are our principal concerns here—emerged out of a review of the failures of the past, out of a process of "taking stock," as it were, of the social and economic symptoms of stagnation. Hence a brief review of some of the literature on labor problems in the period immediately following the Gorbachev accession will set the stage for our examination of the issue of "democratization" of management as it emerged at the end of the 1980s.

The Failure of Prereform Participatory Mechanisms

The highly critical appraisals of prevailing participatory mechanisms that were published in 1985–87 helped prepare the groundwork for the new approaches to worker participation that followed. But it would be a mistake to regard the "official" forms of participation that the authorities had encouraged earlier in the decade as being confined to the obviously "fictitious" kinds of participation celebrated in previous years ("socialist emulation" campaigns, workers' attendance at production conferences). The extension of the work-brigade system in the early 1980s and the enactment of the 1983 Law on the Labor Collective represented attempts to provide a framework for some degree of genuine worker involvement in plant-level decisions.

The organization of industrial work on the basis of brigades or work teams was not a new phenomenon in the Soviet economy. But the early 1980s saw a considerable expansion in this form of work organization (the proportion of industrial workers organized in brigades increased from roughly one-third in 1980 to approximately two-thirds by 1985), with particular stress placed on the growth of those types of brigades that appeared to increase workers' opportunities for shop-floor decision making. Such brigades would be given a single work order or assignment applicable to the brigade as a whole (*edinyi nariad*), with the distribution of job assignments and team earnings among individual members remaining as decisions to be made by the brigade members themselves, not by managerial authorities. Or, at least this was the version of worker participation in brigade decisions that was officially encouraged and enshrined in a new legal statute. The 1983 Law on the Labor Collective explicitly declared that brigade members, either directly or (when the size of the brigade was relatively large, normally understood to mean more than ten members) through a brigade council they elected, "participate in deciding issues of the makeup of the brigade, the planning and organization of its work, the payment and stimulation of labor" (Vedomosti, 1983).

This law not only spelled out the "rights" of work brigades but also contained a number of other provisions allegedly ensuring the implementation of what it immodestly called "genuine socialist self-management." Only some of the more ambitious of such provisions need be cited here. General meetings of the work collectives were "to examine the most important issues of the life and activity" of the work unit. The collective, presumably through such meetings, was to "participate" in working out preliminary versions of economic plans that would then be sent to higher authorities for "ratification." Similarly, the work collective would "participate in deciding" questions of the utilization of incentive funds and funds available for construction of housing and cultural facilities. In the words of one Soviet commentator, the meetings at which such issues would be decided were intended to be "democratic forums" (Il'inskii, 1987, p. 150).

However, one of the striking features of both the "academic" and the "journalistic" literature on labor problems in 1985–87 is the abundant evidence it provides of the failure of the extension of the work-brigade system earlier in the decade, and of the 1983 statute, to produce any noticeable rise in workers' involvement in plant-level decision making. If workers' responses to the questions of inquiring Soviet sociologists on these matters can be taken at face value, the great majority would have reacted favorably to genuine participatory opportunities. Thus less than 10 percent of a sample of workers in a study by Nazimova and Gordon (1986, p. 51) accepted the view that "workers should not interfere in the management of production; this is a matter for the administration." But the enormous gap between workers' apparent readiness to participate and their limited opportunities to do so is suggested by the following summary of a score of empirical studies of the functioning of the work-brigade system in the early 1980s (Gordon, Monusova, and Nazimova, 1987, p. 128):

> Actual practice shows that workers' participation in management through brigades is often based on the prevailing pattern, frequently involving only passive participation in meetings. Brigade councils are by no means always "inserted" in the system of management, . . . and the managerial functions delegated to them are arbitrarily restricted by management. . . . It is also frequently noted that an obstacle to the development of self-management in brigades is the uncertainty of workers concerning its efficacy. Many of them feel that management is not interested in granting workers a real right of management.

Studies conducted by the Soviet trade-union research department confirm this general picture. For example, no more than 13–14 percent of the workers sampled in these studies were involved in "deciding questions of planning and organization of the work of brigades," and similar proportions participated in decisions bearing on the distribution of brigade wages and incentive payments (Shkurko and Meshcherkin, 1987, p. 104). As for the 1983 Law on the Labor Collective and the expectation of some that "democratic forums" at the enterprise would decide major issues of its economic life, here is the judgment of the above-cited trade-union study: "The rights granted by the Law . . . exist to a large degree formally and are essentially used on a very limited scale." Decisions made "above" the brigade level (for example, on the enterprise's economic plan and the allocation of its premium funds) provided even less opportunity for worker involvement than brigade decisions. Thus it is hardly surprising that Gordon and Klopov's study early in 1987 found that only 11 percent of sampled workers felt themselves to be "masters of the enterprise," i.e., felt that they had "an active influence on the state of affairs" at the enterprise, a figure no higher than the findings of a comparable study at the end of the 1970s (compare Nazimova and Gordon, 1986, p. 55, and Gordon and Klopov, 1987, p. 26).

Why the obvious failure of official participatory mechanisms (such as the expanded work-brigade system and the 1983 statute) to generate clear signs of increased employee involvement in workplace decisions? One obstacle, as might be expected, was the resistance of managerial personnel to the threatened reduction of their own authority, or as the trade-union study put it (Shkurko and Meshcherkin, 1987, p. 101), their fear of the weakening of "one-man management" (*edinonachalie*). Another, no less important, obstacle was the inherently limited autonomy of individual economic enterprises in the traditional command system, with output assignments and input allocations determined for the enterprise by higher authorities. What meaning could be attached, under such circumstances, to employee "participation" in formulating the enterprise's economic plan and in deciding on the allocation of funds for cultural and housing facilities? In addition, there were no obvious efforts at this time to reinforce the moderate steps toward "democratization" of management with supportive institutional changes elsewhere in the system. There was nothing to suggest that such "democratization" was part of a broader social and economic process that workers, managers, and political activists should take seriously.

Thus, the unsuccessful attempts in the early 1980s to create a sense of involvement in workplace decisions, and the discussions of these failures that followed, would help make the "democratization" of management a critical part of the reformist agenda later in the decade.

The Theme of Worker Alienation

Beginning in approximately 1986, Soviet discussions of labor problems began to invoke the phenomenon of worker alienation (sometimes explicitly, sometimes implicitly) as a way of supporting the need for enhanced opportunities for worker participation in management. What is of special interest here is the manner in which the meaning attached to the concept of alienation steadily "escalated," so that before long the problem came to be recognized as essentially systemic in nature.

Among the first explicitly to invoke the concept of alienation in these discussions was the sociologist Iu. Riurikov (1986). But for Riurikov the problem was a somewhat narrowly conceived "technological alienation" that impoverished the work process. This was not an alienation rooted in class domination and exploitation (it did not have the "antagonistic character" associated with alienation under capitalism), but it did reflect the kind of extreme division of labor that generates a multitude of highly fragmented, routinized, and monotonous jobs. Such work could not help but produce indifference and passivity on the job. Some of its other consequences, which seemed to be "growing steadily," included poor work discipline, drunkenness, and pilferage on the job. There was one essential antidote to such "technological alienation" for Riurikov. The more impoverished the work process (the less absorbing it was intellectually, physically, "morally"), the more important it was to create opportunities for worker participation in management. This required increased independence in daily "production relations" and—"in deeds, not in words"—opportunities for employees to exercise their right as "masters" or "bosses" of their own labor. There was no effort by Riurikov to specify the particular mechanisms that would create such opportunities. But the general thrust of the argument was clear: increased scope for participation in managerial decision making as an offset to the technologically induced impoverishment of work content.

Views essentially similar to those of Riurikov were sometimes expressed without explicitly invoking the concept of alienation. One such example appeared in the writings of G. Rakitskaia (1986). For this economist the normal production process in Soviet society "constantly breeds a tendency toward a peculiar kind of technological despotism," a situation in which the individual functions as a partial, one-sided, underdeveloped worker. Once again, as in Riurikov's formulation, these consequences can be overcome through a system of "democratic management" that provides sufficient scope for the development of those personal capacities that the work process alone inhibits. But there was an essential difference between these two writers. For Riurikov there was apparently no alternative to the application of inherently "alienating" technology at the current stage of economic development. Its negative consequences for the work experience could only be mitigated once it was introduced. For Rakitskaia the Soviet economy had reached a point where choices among alternative technologies were available with increasing frequency. Where this was the case, the choice should be guided by "social criteria of effectiveness." Although the precise content of the "social criteria" was not specified by Rakitskaia, the general meaning of the concept was fairly obvious. Where alternative technologies are available, choice should be made with due regard for minimizing the consequences of "technological despotism" (or Riurikov's "technological alienation"), that is, fragmented, routinized, impoverished work content. As for already installed technology, there was always some room for the application of the "democratic variant of the management of labor."

The somewhat rhetorical nature of these formulations should not obscure the fact that something quite new—at least in the Soviet context—was being said here. Both the choice of technology and the implementation of "democratic management" should be guided by the "priority of social criteria of effectiveness over economic ones."[1] We shall return to the larger significance of these "social criteria" when we consider some of the additional literature on workplace "democratization" in the section below.

More recent discussions of alienation have substantially extended its meaning and applicability to Soviet circumstances. The philosophical literature (Blium, 1987) explicitly rejected the formerly dominant view that symptoms of alienation represented merely "survivals" of the past or "birthmarks" of the new society and that "alienation in no way arises from the essence and nature of socialist relation." It was now seen as permeating Soviet society. How else to explain, asked a critic of the older view (ibid.), the indifference of producers to the product of their work, the failure of workers to perceive themselves as "in charge" or "masters" of their work activity, the phenomena of consumerism and political apathy? What is it, asked this critic, "in actually existing socialist economic and sociopolitical relations that generates alienation?"

At least a partial response to this question—a response suggesting the systemic roots of worker alienation—was provided by the sociologist R. Ryvkina (1987). It had essentially nothing to do with "technological alienation" or the concepts invoked in the apologetics ("survivals" and "birthmarks") of the older Soviet philosophical literature on alienation. Ryvkina reported the results of an empirical study of several state enterprises in which extremely large proportions of employees (75–90 percent) admitted to working well below their capacity. Why? Perhaps the principal source of this behavior, in Ryvkina's view, was the concentration of the right to make decisions on organizational, financial, and personnel issues in the hands of the "official apparatus." Employees commonly received directions "from above" that they regarded as mistaken or pointless but that they implemented because "what else is one to do." The work rules or instructions that guided their behavior were clearly not regarded as "their own." Very rarely (in only some 5–7 percent of the cases) were appeals to revoke what employees regarded as mistaken or pointless instructions responded to in positive terms. For Ryvkina the meaning of these and other similar findings was unambiguous: They pointed to the "alienation of working people from property" and from "the system within which they functioned." Hence the "indifference toward work, the low level of involvement, the low quality of work and of produced output."

In this situation, the implementation of elections of economic executives would certainly be a step in the right direction, but no less important for Ryvkina was the need to affirm and encourage the development of a certain value system "for each one of us." Among the most desirable values was a readiness to intervene actively in decision making on "production questions," up to the point of exerting pressure on "the leadership" and even of a "confrontation" with it. Another such value was that of not being satisfied with whatever level of power and independence one had already attained in the work situation but of striving to extend it. An underlying theme in Ryvkina's discussion here was the need for "pressure from below" on those with authority.

Thus, quite apart from its "technological" sources, alienation was now recognized as being rooted in the highly unequal distribution of authority over workplace decisions, and the urgency of extending opportunities to participate in such decisions could even justify "confrontation" with one's superiors. Readers with even the slightest knowledge of traditional Soviet managerial ideology will surely recognize the considerable distance that had been traversed in a relatively short time.[2]

Principal Justifications for "Democratization"

The explicit acknowledgment of the ineffectiveness of prevailing participatory mechanisms, and the readiness to admit the existence of widespread worker alienation, obviously contributed to making the need for workplace reform a major public issue in the years immediately following the Gorbachev accession. But the chief function served by most of the literature just reviewed was to expose and document the problem of worker passivity rather than to elaborate the case for the "democratization" of management. When we turn to the writings whose principal concern was explicitly to justify such "democratization," we encounter a considerable range of arguments and concepts.

In their crudest, "minimalist" version, Soviet arguments for participation in management have always seen it as essentially a means of promoting "initiative from below" for the purpose of finding and utilizing production "reserves" at the workplace, i.e., opportunities for enhancing the productive performance of the enterprise with available resources (Zolotov, 1987). While Soviet justifications for worker participation (or "democratization" of management) almost never ignore the presumed positive impact on worker productivity, one way of gauging the seriousness and novelty of recent Soviet discussions of this subject is by noting how far they have moved beyond this "minimalist" version. Let us consider three arguments that have appeared in the literature since 1986.

1. One of these is already familiar to us. In 1986–87 L. Gordon and his colleagues reiterated and elaborated the theme that appeared in their writings earlier in the decade (see chapter 1): The effective utilization of the new scientific-industrial technology had made worker participation in management a "production necessity" (Nazimova and Gordon, 1986; Gordon, Klopov, and Petrov, 1987). The principal characteristics associated with the new technology—the large share of jobs involving the processing and transmission of information, the frequent need to confront "nonstandard operations," the "permanent mobility, flexibility, and variability" of production processes (Gordon, Klopov, and Petrov, 1987, p. 7)—place a premium on workers' ability to make independent decisions. Put somewhat differently, they require changing the relative importance of "centralism and democratic principles" in favor of the latter (Gordon and Nazimova,

1986, p. 13). At least on the surface there was an essential similarity between this justification for "democratization" and what we have called the "minimalist" version. In both cases the desirability of enhanced worker involvement in management decisions rests largely on its expected positive impact on enterprise economic performance.[3] In this sense such involvement is essentially an instrumental value, not an end in itself. But in a departure from the primitive instrumentalism characteristic of the traditional "minimalist" version, Gordon recognized that meaningful worker participation could not become a reality unless it was one element of a general economic reform that significantly increased enterprise autonomy. Furthermore, the implementation of such autonomy would make worker participation in management "socially necessary" (Gordon, Klopov, and Petrov, 1987, p. 10). That is, it would be obviously undesirable to "reduce" enterprise independence to the independence of professional managers.

2. A somewhat different case for workplace "democratization" initially emerged from Zaslavskaia's elaboration of the concept of the "human factor." The concept was developed in such a way as to highlight its contrast with the traditional Soviet view of the "role of man" in the production process (Zaslavskaia, 1986, pp. 10–17).[4] In the latter view, the role of human beings was identified with their functioning as "labor resources." But for Zaslavskaia, this view of people "as labor resources means equating them with such material and physical factors of production as machinery, raw materials, energy, etc." Like other such resources, they were passive in nature and had to be treated as essentially "objects of management." Such a view of people's role in production was associated with a relatively narrow conception of the kinds of needs that had to be met in order to generate adequate work effort from these "labor resources." Such needs (or what Zaslavskaia called the correspondingly narrow conception of "social tasks") were confined to "securing the normal conditions of reproduction of labor resources," i.e., essentially improved supplies of consumer necessities, housing facilities, medical care, etc. While all of this was obviously nec-

essary, it was insufficient to mobilize the "social energy" required to accelerate economic growth. Stated in the most general terms, Zaslavskaia's alternative conception of the "human factor" stressed the role of the work force as—at least potentially—the "active agent" in the production process. Perhaps the most critical point was that workers' needs included not only improved supplies of essential consumer goods but also those needs encompassed by a correspondingly broader conception of "social tasks," i.e., the provision of "accurate social and political information, political and economic democracy, social respect, interesting contacts, and an intensive intellectual life." More concretely, this meant that the satisfaction of such needs—and thus the mobilization of heightened work effort—required the creation of workplace relationships that would grant workers real "disposal over the means of production," that would create a sense of their being "in charge" (*chuvstvo khoziaina*), even if this applied only to the particular work section in which they were employed.

This broader, "human-factor" conception of workers' needs and what is necessary to satisfy them has been repeatedly invoked since 1986 to justify what Soviet writers have begun to call industrial democracy. For A.B. Veber, for example, the favorable impact of the latter on economic performance is confirmed by Western studies that reveal a positive correlation between the extent of unionization and productive efficiency. Insofar as unions are able to function as channels for the expression of the "collective voice" of workers, they reflect a form of industrial democracy and its capacity to mobilize the "human factor" in the production process (Veber, 1988).[5] For V.I. Gerchikov (1989, p. 34) such a mobilization is possible only through "the profound democratization of the relations of production," a process that entails the transfer to workers of some of the functions, rights, and responsibilities of "bosses" or "proprietors" (*khoziaeva*). While these formulations often remain rather general, at the very least it is clear that the rhetoric of industrial democracy has begun to permeate Soviet discussions of labor problems.

As in the case of Gordon and his colleagues, here too the general case for workplace democratization rests largely on its expected favorable impact on economic indices. But for Zaslavskaia this appears to be essentially a short-run consideration. In the long run, the growth of the country's economic potential (its "productive forces") must be regarded as a means to the attainment of a higher level of "social relations" and to the improvement of "man himself" (Zaslavskaia, 1986, p. 13). This appears to be Zaslavskaia's way of asserting the primacy of "social" over "economic" goals, with democratization of value mainly in its own right rather than as an instrument for accelerating economic growth—but only in the long run.

3. Perhaps the most interesting—certainly the most challenging—defense of workplace "democratization" has been offered by those who see it as having positive spillover effects on the larger society. While critically important, increased opportunities for worker participation represent only one aspect of a much needed broader process of democratization of the economy and society. Some of the writings of the economist B. Rakitskii appear to provide the clearest expression of this position. For Rakitskii, a principal objective of ongoing reformist efforts must be radically to change the "relations between the managers and the managed" (1987). However, the context here is not purely economic. The process he has in mind ("democratization") would require the active involvement of working people in deciding not only strictly production problems but, "above all, sociopolitical and state issues." The same kind of all-embracing formulation accompanies Rakitskii's argument that people's interests and involvement in public affairs can be adequately mobilized only if "all decisions, without exception, are made in a democratic way. This must mean real access for all and for each to participate in the preparation of decisions" (ibid.). Rakitskii's celebration of democratic decision making is extended to the economic sphere in a similarly comprehensive manner. "All of economics is permeated with the need to make the best choice among alternatives" (ibid.). But the critical issue is who makes

the choice? In a system of "command-and-pressure management" (*komandno-nazhimnoe upravlenie*), it is made by those with the power to command. The result is that some possibilities are excluded, and even desirable choices remain unimplemented. But there is a better way: "Democratization will permit everyone to really participate in the optimization of economic decisions beginning with his own job, the work section, the shop, and ending up with the affairs of the economy as a whole" (ibid.).

Rakitskii also anticipated the objections of those who might wonder whether democratization, especially at the workplace, is compatible with the kind of discipline required for efficient production. Can self-imposed "voluntary discipline" alone be relied upon when some workers are unavoidably assigned unpleasant, low-prestige job functions? The hypothetical case cited by Rakitskii in response to this question may seem oversimplified, but it was obviously formulated so as to stress the transforming potential that worker participation in management could have both in the workplace and beyond it (ibid.):

> Imagine that the [unpleasant] task is assigned to a worker who, together with his comrades in the shop and the enterprise, has already discussed the problems of organizing work and production, and together they have determined how ... to restructure things so as to eliminate the undesirable and nonprestigious jobs. This is already another kind of worker. . . . He is not confined by the boundaries of his workplace. He is not only a factor in the fulfillment of the plan but also a human being thinking about problems of production and society, and how to change them for the better.

Rakitskii was not alone in elaborating the theme of worker participation as a possible spur to the democratization of the larger society. Here is how several participants at a conference on workers' self-management early in 1988 formulated the case for what might be called the "external effects" of enhanced worker involvement in decision making on the job: "self-management, by coming into conflict in the course of its development with prevailing economic and political structures, can become one of the principal impulses (*dvigateli*) to radical economic reform and political democratization. . . . Perhaps this is only a small chance, but it should be utilized" (Kudiukin, 1988, pp. 46–47). However, more recent discussions of the relationship between democratization within the workplace and outside it have clearly recognized that the prospects for the former are critically dependent on "general social and political reforms" (Rakitskaia and Rakitskii, 1988, p. 20), i.e., on democratization of the political and social environment outside the workplace.

The various arguments for democratization of management reviewed above reflect not so much conflicting points of view as differences in emphasis. They tend to reinforce one another rather than to cancel one another. But they do exhibit the same kind of expansionary logic that has characterized so many other areas of Soviet reformist discourse. Thus what was formerly a rather modest appeal for increased opportunities for worker involvement in shop-floor decisions has more recently evolved into demands for the "real access of working people to management at all its levels" (Rakitskaia, 1989, p. 41). Moreover, as already noted, the economic (productivity-enhancing) impact of increased worker participation is no longer its only—or even its principal—justification. The democratization of management has come to be linked with the notion of subordinating the economy to "humanistic" and "sociopolitical" ends (ibid., pp. 41–42). But all of these formulations are essentially statements of general principles. How are they related to the actual institutional mechanisms governing labor–management relations that have been introduced in recent years?

What specific forms has the democratization of management taken in the framework of the new institutional mechanisms? To what extent has such democratization become a reality rather than merely a formal facade? What kinds of controversies have emerged on the general issue of implementing the democratization of management? These are some of the questions confronted below.

A New Legal Framework and
Managerial Elections

We have seen that the simple issuance of a new Soviet statute providing for expanded "self-management" (the 1983 Law on Labor Collectives, for example) need have no significant impact on actual opportunities for employee participation in management. But it obviously does not follow that any conceivable statute in this area is fated to be similarly ineffective. Much will depend on accompanying changes in the political and economic environment within which it is administered. At the very least, the Law on the State Enterprise (henceforth cited as the State Enterprise Law), which went into effect at the beginning of 1988, signaled the formal institutionalization of several new participatory mechanisms. While it is clearly too early to pronounce any final judgments on the practical impact of the statute, there are some grounds for the view that it may have had a significant impact on participatory opportunities. Indeed, it began to have some impact even before it was officially instituted at the start of 1988. A preliminary version of the statute was issued for "public discussion" early in 1987, and reports of its "experimental" application (in anticipation of its final authorization) began to appear shortly thereafter. Our review of the discussions and practices associated with this statute, in the period immediately preceding and following its formal introduction in January 1988, will demonstrate that the theory and practice of worker participation in the Soviet Union have already moved well beyond the levels reached in earlier years. But we are also interested in signs of resistance to the participatory mechanisms as well as in indications that some participants in these discussions were prepared to go further than the new statute explicitly authorized.

The State Enterprise Law provided for the "election" of various categories of managerial personnel, ranging from brigade leaders and foremen to plant directors. In its final (but not in its preliminary) version, it specified that such elections should be carried out "as a rule on a competitive basis." The law endowed the "labor collective" of the enterprise with the power to resolve "all questions of production and social development" independently. The general meeting of the collective "is the basic form of exercising the labor collective's authority." In the period between meetings of the collective, its authority was to be exercised by an elected assembly—the council of the labor collective (referred to henceforth as the work council). No more than a quarter of this council could consist of management representatives. At the same time, the law affirmed the applicability of the principle of "one-man management." (We leave for later the attempts of Soviet writers to reconcile "one-man management" with the presumed authority of the elected work councils.) These provisions of the statute are summarized here so that the reader can make better sense of our account of Soviet discussions of workplace procedures that continued since it was originally issued.

But there is an additional key feature of the 1988 Enterprise Law that must be explicitly recognized. The law not only spelled out the participatory mechanisms associated with the "democratization" of management. It also embodied the main principles of the general economic reform introduced at the same time. In other words, unlike the 1983 Law on the Labor Collective, the new participatory mechanisms were to be reinforced by projected increases in enterprise autonomy. The "control figures" handed down to individual enterprises were to serve as "guidelines" rather than as obligatory assignments. Enterprises were "independently" to work out and confirm their own plans.

Clearly, the new State Enterprise Law marked a turning point in Soviet policy on worker participation. As might be expected, one of the principal issues raised in the course of the discussions and early applications of the law was that of managerial elections.

Although most of the initial published reactions to the new law supported the general principle of election of managerial personnel, some participants in these discussions obviously sought to limit the applicability of the principle. This was most clearly expressed in repeated warnings (especially by local party officials) that there were still many "immature" or "unhealthy" work collectives that could not be trusted to elect "principled" executives. As some particularly vigilant observers of poor work habits put it, "under the flag of democracy" some workers who were used to being forgiven for drinking and slipshod work would try to retain in managerial positions those who forgave them. In some cases such warnings were accompanied by proposals that the State Enterprise Law be modified to permit the "appointment" of managers in exceptional situations. In other cases those who doubted the "maturity" of worker–electors seemed prepared to rely on the party's powers of persuasion to help elect the most competent managers (Morozov and Sorokin, 1987; Postal'nyi, 1987; Artemev and Illarionov, 1987). But the frequency with which such warnings were published in the months following the issuance of the preliminary version of the State Enterprise Law suggests considerable resistance to the general idea of managerial elections. This may help explain an interesting modification included in the election provisions of the final version of the law. If the candidate elected to the position of chief executive of the enterprise is not confirmed by the "higher-level agency," a new election must be held. Thus without abandoning the general principle of managerial elections, some limits were placed on the negative consequences of the choices that might be made by "immature" work collectives.

But both before and after the final version of the law went into effect there was no shortage of responses to those who stressed the dangers of allowing "immature" work groups to select managerial personnel. Thus a strong supporter of the electoral principle (Torkanovskii, 1988b, p. 56) observed that those party officials and managers who warned that some work collectives were "not ready for elections" typically judged employees' readiness by the degree to which the latter's probable choices corresponded to their own, i.e., to the views of the "apparatus." In the same spirit, another defender of elections writing in an organ of the party's Central Committee noted, "People simply do not want to accept a situation in which issues affecting their interests are decided without their participation" (Petrik, 1987, p. 65). While it was certainly possible that the work collective might be mistaken in choosing as manager someone other than the candidate supported by the party organization, it was "altogether possible that the majority will be wiser and more far sighted" (ibid., p. 63). Still another supporter of the electoral principle warned that the greater danger stemmed not from the "spontaneity of freedom" (surely another way of pointing to the alleged danger of relying on the choices of "immature" work collectives) but from a return to the "command" methods of the past (Krasnov, 1988b, p. 109).

Moreover, if the general principle of managerial elections was to be taken seriously, the electoral process at enterprises would have to be made more credible than it had generally been in the society at large. A commentary on the traditional Soviet electoral process readily admitted that it was "close to absurd and long discredited" (Khallik, 1987, p. 21). Another article characterized the familiar practice of nominating a single candidate for elective posts as "the principal method of profaning the idea of elections in our history" (Gerchikov and Proshkin, 1988, p. 96). Published reports began to appear describing multiple-candidate elections to executive positions in writers' organizations, local soviets, and city government (*Literaturnaia gazeta*, October 21, 1987; Strashun, 1987; Vodovozov and Novikov, 1988). Clearly, there was a certain logic to the modifying phrase incorporated into the final version of the State Enterprise Law: Elections of enterprise executives are to be conducted "as a rule on a competitive basis." Thus, in its final form the new law—like so much else in Soviet public life in 1987–88—reflected the conflicting pressures emanating from both conservatives and reformers. Election results could be undone by "higher-level agencies," but multiple-candidate elections were to be encouraged.

It would certainly be surprising if the initial prospect of managerial elections, followed by their statutory implementation beginning in early 1988, did not generate considerable skepticism and some outright opposition on the part of certain social groups. Factory party officials accustomed to—at the very least—"ap-

proving" new managerial appointments and higher-level managerial personnel accustomed to selecting their subordinates could
hardly be expected to welcome the possibility of anything approximating genuine elections. Indeed, as might be expected,
several sociological studies have found clear evidence of substantial opposition by managerial personnel to the general principle of elections, except when the latter are confined to choosing
foremen or brigade leaders. One of the conclusions of a survey
conducted by the National Public Opinion Research Center
(Kapeliush, 1989, p. 11) undoubtedly reflected a common situation: the higher the official job status of respondents, the greater
the opposition to elections of managers. But it would be an obvious mistake to assume that the self-interested concerns of those
whose powers would be threatened or reduced by managerial
elections were the only source of opposition to the new procedure. Clearly, there were perfectly legitimate "objective" grounds
for questioning the appropriateness of such elections in a society
unaccustomed to choosing its leaders freely in any area of economic or political life. Of all things, why start with elections of
managers?

The issue was posed directly by A. Migranian (Roundtable,
1989a, p. 76): "I am puzzled by the increasingly resolute transition to the principle of elections of administrators at all levels of
management. Without the tradition and experience of democratic
elections in the political sphere, we have decided immediately to
thrust ourselves 'ahead of the whole planet' in the sphere of
industrial democracy." Migranian's reasoning here illustrates
how Western experience and traditions could be invoked as an
argument against the introduction of managerial elections. That
experience demonstrated, in his view, that democratic forms appropriate to the political sphere could not be "mechanically transferred" to the economic sphere. The need to rely on "professionalism," especially in selecting higher-level managers, seemed
clearly to limit the applicability of the electoral principle.

Even those Soviet commentators who sought to respond directly to Migranian acknowledged that he had posed a genuine

problem, namely, how to reconcile "economic democracy" with the need for a high level of professional competence among managers. But for S. Peregudov, invoking Western experience could not be regarded as persuasive (ibid.). The absence of employee involvement in managerial elections in the West reflected primarily the nonowner status of such employees rather than their limited capacity to assess managerial competence. Peregudov's main concern was that Soviet managerial elections could become discredited (a mere "game" of democracy) unless the range of independent decisions that could be made at the enterprise level was substantially enlarged. G. Diligenskii's response to Migranian (ibid., p. 77) stressed the potential impact that managerial elections could have on "the development of a mass democratic consciousness." In a particular version of what we earlier called the "spillover-effect" argument for workplace democratization, Diligenskii pointed to the positive role that managerial elections could have in overcoming the passivity of the masses and in stimulating "their interest in independent and active participation in public affairs." Quite apart from these explicit responses to Migranian, two basic arguments in defense of managerial elections appeared repeatedly in the more serious literature on this subject in 1988–89 (Gerchikov and Proshkin, 1988; Gerchikov, 1989): (1) an elected manager, functioning as "a leader invested with voluntary trust," would be in a position to place higher demands on the workers under him than an officially appointed administrator; and (2) a manager elected by the collective, and thus capable of acting in its name, would be better able to resist arbitrary demands and pressures "from above." Thus, whatever the motivations of those who succeeded in incorporating the electoral principle in the 1988 State Enterprise Law, the early period of its implementation witnessed a lively exchange between skeptics[6] and defenders of managerial elections, an exchange, moreover, that exhibited greater maturity and balance than might have been expected at this stage in the discussion of a comparatively novel idea.

This period also saw the emergence of what might loosely be

termed "approved" or—in a more ambitious version—"ideal" electoral procedures. These were the features of recent elections that received the most favorable commentary in published reports, or the practices that were explicitly recommended as appropriate for the future. Perhaps the closest approach to an ideal model of such procedures was formulated by Gerchikov and Proshkin (1988, p. 95): "In our view, the basic principles of elections of managers are a mandatory secret ballot, the presence of several candidates for the position, the necessity for the candidates themselves to work out their own election programs, and openness and democratic procedures in nominating candidates." The need to implement the first and last of these principles seemed particularly urgent to these commentators. Reliance on the secret ballot should be "virtually absolute," and any member of the work collective should have the right to nominate a candidate up to the time of the actual voting. As for the principle of multiple candidates, while its implementation should certainly be the rule ("we paid dearly" for its absence in the past), certain exceptions could be recognized as legitimate. Thus, where the election involved a relatively low-status managerial position—presumably brigade leader or foreman—or where there was apparently universal agreement that a particular candidate was unquestionably superior to all possible alternatives, to insist on formally implementing the principle of multiple candidates would only help to discredit elections.[7]

The issue of eligible voters also required clarification, and here, too, Gerchikov and Proshkin, among others, contributed to the formulation of what might be regarded as the "approved" procedures. In elections to lower-level managerial positions (brigade leader, foreman, section chief), eligible voters should normally include all employees in the affected unit (brigade, section, etc.). In voting for higher-level positions (plant director, shop chief), especially in large plants, the prevailing view seemed to be that eligible "electors" should be confined to elected representatives drawn from the various departments and work brigades in the plant or should include only those who would be "immediate subordinates" of the future incumbent. However, the exact procedure to be followed in such cases—including the possibility of extending voting privileges to all employees—should be decided by the work collective itself (Gerchikov and Proshkin, 1988, pp. 100–101). In one highly publicized election for plant director of a Latvian enterprise—apparently intended to serve as a model—"electors" included 10 percent of the staff of some 4,000 employees (Sungorkin, 1987). In another plant with 750 employees, voting "delegates" numbered 106 (Konstantinov, 1987).

To fill vacancies for top-level managerial positions in relatively large enterprises, advertisements might be placed in local or national newspapers. In such cases it would be appropriate for an "electoral commission" (comprising representatives of the plant's party organization, technical specialists, and perhaps ministry representatives) to select the two or three candidates presented to the electors from the mass of applicants for the position. The plant's party organization should not "stand aside" during the course of these elections, but it should also "not impose its candidate" on the work collective (Morozov, 1988, p. 58).

While there are some ambiguities here (the decision on eligible voters, for example), it is nonetheless much easier to identify the principal features of this "approved" or popularized version of appropriate election procedures than to assess the degree to which they have actually been implemented. The problem is the abundance of conflicting evidence. On the one hand, there was no shortage of published accounts in 1987–89 describing cases of multicandidate elections for managerial positions (Konstantinov, 1987; Kozlov, 1987; Morozov, 1988; Ershova, 1988; Loshak, 1989; Komilev, 1989). Moreover, these accounts frequently included the "box scores," or voting results, showing each of the competing candidates receiving a substantial percentage of votes cast. But how representative were such published reports of typical managerial selection procedures? In summing up press accounts of procedures followed in selecting new managerial personnel in 1987 (when "experiments" in managerial elections were being encouraged, although the State Enterprise Law had not yet gone into effect), Torkanovskii concluded that only "1–2 percent were chosen in a really democratic manner" (1988b, p. 56). But even after the law took effect (January 1988), an abundance of published reports continued to appear documenting the violation of normal election procedures. One illustration, drawn from the Donetsk region, is typical of other such reports (Iakimenko, 1989, p. 55): "Elections of managerial personnel are proceeding timidly, in most cases through open voting, and very often with a single candidate. It does not appear that the command system is an agony, and workers understand this very well."[8]

On the basis of the evidence available to us, the most that can be concluded is that by the end of the 1980s the first steps had been taken toward legitimizing the idea of subordinates' participation in the election of managerial personnel. These steps included the provision of a new legal framework for such elections, the elaboration and popularization of democratic procedures as appropriate in the selection of managers (the "approved" version described above), and the generally positive portrayal in the press of what appeared to be genuinely competitive elections for managerial positions. But it is also clear that such elections had by no means become the norm. Indeed, they were probably the exception.[9] Nonetheless, it is worth noting that the principle of competitive elections was affirmed—certainly in theory and to a limited degree in practice—in the context of choosing plant management before it was implemented in the choice of deputies to the Congress of People's Deputies in March 1989.

"One-Man Management" and Work Councils

Actual managerial behavior in the Soviet Union is obviously not a simple reflection of "official" managerial ideology, but it is certainly influenced by it. Hence the importance of identifying certain recent changes in the prevailing ideology of management.

One important feature of these changes has been the modification or weakening (but not the abrogation) of the traditional principle of one-man management. This process has taken a variety of forms.

One of the themes that began to appear in the management literature of the late 1980s was that one-man management "must have its limits" (Krasnov, 1988a). It should not be "absolutized" (Ivanov, 1987, p. 64). After all, there were cases, "and not so rare at that," in which the directives of the manager may reflect "group" or "bureaucratic" interests rather than the interests of the work collective and the state (Maslennikov, 1987, p. 55). Similar sentiments were expressed in the appeal to abandon certain stereotypes that had functioned to instill a "respect for power." Among the most widespread of these stereotypes were the notions that "he who has more rights is right" and "one-man management is more important than democracy" (Chichilimov, 1987). Authoritative voices began to be heard proclaiming the very opposite of the latter proposition. Thus, for Iu. A. Tikhomirov the time had come to implement "a new relationship between one-man management and collegiality in which the latter has priority" (1988, p. 132).

None of these formulations signified that the principle of one-man management had been explicitly repudiated. Indeed, as noted earlier, the final version of the Law on the State Enterprise (1987) unambiguously reaffirmed it (Article 6, par. 4): "Within the bounds of the enterprise's jurisdiction, its executive issues orders and instructions that are binding for all employees of the enterprise. The decisions of executives of structural units and subdivisions and of foremen and brigade leaders are binding for all employees subordinate to them."

But the same document also provided that the decisions of an elected council of the labor collective (no more than a fourth of whose members could be managerial personnel) were "binding for management and the members of the collective." How could the "democratization of management," presumably embodied in the principle of an elected employees' council (referred to below as work council) exercising the "powers of the labor collective," be reconciled with the principle of one-man management (or, as some have put it, with the need for "professionalism" in management)? Some of the recent literature that explicitly confronted this problem distinguished between "strategic," "long-run," and "social-development" issues on the one hand, and "operational" and "current" matters (the direct "organization of the production process") on the other. Decisions on the former set of issues were to be subject to the approval of the collective's work council, while decisions on the latter fell within the domain of one-man management (Torkanovskii, 1987, 1988a; Krasnov, 1988a; Merzlikina, 1989). Thus, the allocation of the enterprise's net income among capital investment, employees' bonuses, and out-lays on housing would become the prerogative of the council. This did not mean, of course, that management should simply ignore these matters but that its proposals in these areas had to obtain the approval of the collective's council. If management failed to persuade the council of the correctness of its proposed course of action, "it is a bad decision" and must be withdrawn (Roundtable, 1987). Moreover, at least in the view of one commentator, a "confrontation" between an enterprise manager and the council reflected badly on the manager, not on the employees. It was a "result of his inability or unwillingness to reject command-administrative methods, evidence of the unfitness of the executive to perform managerial functions under the new conditions of economic management" (Torkanovskii, 1987, p. 54).

Changes in Soviet managerial ideology were also reflected in the metaphors and analogies that began to be commonly invoked to characterize the new relationship that should prevail between an enterprise's top executives and its work collective (or the collective's representative body—its work council). The common theme of these characterizations was the dependent status of the former relative to the latter. For example: "The distribution of functions between management and agencies of self-management [the work councils] is similar to the distribution of functions between the captain of a ship and its owners" (Katul'skii and Kobiakov, 1988, p. 68). In a similar spirit, another observer suggested ("if such analogies are permissible") that the new relationship between the work collective and its executive was comparable to that between "the shareholders of a firm and its manager, who is obliged to organize production in an optimal manner." The work collective endows the executive with the necessary authority but retains for itself "the right to check and assess the results of his activity, and if necessary to remove him from his position" (Krasnov, 1988a, p. 58). A particularly direct and challenging formulation of the anticipated reversal of roles was offered by Torkanovskii: "As for the director, he becomes the executor of the will of the work collective, the representative of its interests in [dealings with] state agencies, and not the other way around, as was the case in the years of the sway of the bureaucratic system" (1988b, p. 51). Another formulation repeatedly invoked to characterize the enhanced authority of the elected work councils referred to them as "parliamentary" or "legislative" organs entrusted with the responsibility of adopting decisions on the principal economic and social issues of the life of the collective. The proper role of enterprise management, on the other hand, was that of an "executive organ" fully accountable to the collective, whose chief function was to implement the decisions "democratically" arrived at by the collective or its "legislative" body (Merzlikina, 1989, pp. 57–59; Perlamutrov, 1989, p. 39). The principle of one-man management, although obviously limited, would continue in force since it was expected that the instructions issued by management in the course of implementing the work collective's decisions would be binding on employees.

It should be stressed that none of these formulations of the proper relationship between professional management and the work councils were intended as descriptions of an already existing state of affairs. Rather, they were statements of objectives, of conditions required to implement the "democratization of management" (or "production democracy"), a goal that clearly remained to be achieved.

Since the elected work council was formally recognized as the principal agency of "self-management" at the enterprise, the issue of the composition and leadership of these bodies assumed considerable importance. Like the general issue of managerial elections (are workers sufficiently "mature" to elect competent managers?), these matters also became the subject of debate. Indeed, some of the striking departures from traditional Soviet views on the distribution of authority at the workplace received a hearing in the course of discussions on the nature of these work councils.

At many of the enterprises that began to "experiment" with the State Enterprise Law before its provisions formally took effect in January 1988, plant directors were selected as chairmen of work councils (councils "elected" their chairmen from among their own members). This was not a difficult result to achieve since plant management and the plant's party organization often presented the principal candidates for membership on the council and for its chairmanship. As defenders of this practice put it, the issue was not that of "retaining power" for directors but of drawing on people with the most experience in decision making and with relatively high levels of "economic education." Besides, as one director put it (Roundtable, 1987), "isn't the function of being chairman of the council of the work collective too complicated for a worker?" Supporters of worker–chairmen (or at least of chairmen drawn from some category other than top management) were also in evidence in these discussions, although it is by no means clear that their position was being adopted as frequently as that of their opponents.

In February 1988 the Soviet trade-union leadership and the State Committee on Labor and Social Issues published a set of recommendations concerning election procedures at economic enterprises (*Ekonomicheskaia gazeta*, 1988, no. 9). One of these recommendations explicitly urged that top executives not be elected to the position of work council chairmen. But in contrast to the situation that would have prevailed in earlier years—when the issuance of such recommendations would have been regarded as a statement of "official" policy, thus ending further discussion of the issue—both proponents and opponents of plant directors as council chairmen continued to be heard. Moreover, it would be something of an oversimplification to characterize supporters of these contrasting positions as invariably conservatives and reformers, respectively.

Thus, shortly after these recommendations were issued, B. Kurashvili, long identified as a principal intellectual spokesman for economic and political reform, questioned the wisdom of blocking top management executives from access to the position of work council chairman. The "key to democratizing the economic mechanism" was the removal of constraints on the economic independence of the enterprise. "Superdemocratization" of internal self-management at the enterprise would not help. Kurashvili appeared to imply that a plant director who was simultaneously chairman of the work council would be in a stronger position to resist "planning by decree, which still prevails, if in a slightly modified form" (1988a).

But for most participants in the discussion that followed there was something obviously incongruous about designating plant directors as heads of bodies designed to implement "democratization of management" at the enterprise. Thus, for M. Krasnov the "very presence" of the director would have a "negative impact" on the other members of the work council. Why? The "stereotypes confirmed by long years of bureaucratic centralism" remained too powerful. The views of the "boss" would necessarily dominate the council. Hence "the requirements of genuine democratization of economic life are hardly compatible with having the top executive . . . become the head of the council" (Krasnov, 1988a, pp. 58–59). Another adherent of this position invoked the findings of sociological studies that appeared to demonstrate that only a small proportion of enterprise directors (10–16 percent) recognized the need "to develop democracy in production." Hence the danger that some work councils ("especially those in which the director is chairman") might be reduced to rubber-stamping management decisions (Torkanovskii, 1988b, p. 53). Furthermore, an "independent" work council would be in a stronger position to perform the vital protective function of resisting the intervention ("which is by no means always competent") of higher-level state agencies and party organizations in the economic affairs of the enterprise. Indeed, for Torkanovskii (1988a; 1988b, pp. 52, 55), not only was it generally undesirable for the director to be simultaneously head of the work council, but it would not necessarily be a "catastrophe" if the director and secretary of a plant's party organization failed to be elected as ordinary members of the work council. This is precisely what happened at a plant cited by Torkanovskii in which the number of candidates for council seats exceeded the number of vacancies and the election was conducted by secret ballot—procedures that this observer strongly endorsed.

No less forthright in their advocacy of independent work councils that would be free of the undue influence of both management personnel and the enterprise's party organization were two economists at Moscow State University, A. Buzgalin and A. Kolganov (1989). In their view, not only should top-level managers and heads of "social organizations" (the party, Komsomol, and trade union) be excluded from access to the chairmanship of work councils; it would even be a mistake to "automatically" include them as ordinary members of such councils. The "conservative" response (here the "conservative" characterization is surely appropriate) was not long in coming. Nor is it surprising that, at least in one of its versions, it came from a representative of Soviet trade unions (Shkurko, 1989). How could an organ of self-management (the work council) function effectively without including representatives of "leading organizations"? In Shkurko's view, the "party bureau, the trade-union committee, the Komsomol bureau," as well as management should "necessarily be represented" on the work councils (ibid., p. 50). It hardly seems necessary to stress the enormous contrast between the conception of independent work councils as organs of self-management that "cannot be subordinate to anyone other than the collective" (Merzlikina, 1989, p. 57) and the view that such councils must "necessarily" include representatives of familiar "leading organizations."

As for the actual functioning of work councils since 1988, the dominant note in the serious labor literature is that plant management has by and large exercised substantial control over the composition and activities of these councils.[10] To the extent that they have had some influence on the state of affairs at the enterprise, it has typically been in the form of "advisory" or "consultative" rather than decision-making functions (Gerchikov, 1989, pp. 37–38). But it is also clear that workers have on occasion sought to resist management and party domination of work councils. This resistance has taken the form of a refusal to elect top management personnel and party and trade-union representatives to the work councils. How frequently this has occurred remains unclear, but some Soviet sources suggest that "many collectives" have acted in this way, particularly when a secret ballot has been available for elections of work-council members (Shkurko, 1989, p. 50; Auzan, 1989, p. 43). Indeed, it was precisely such independent voting behavior that a conservative spokesman cited to justify his insistence—as noted earlier—that certain familiar figures should "necessarily" be included as members of work councils. However limited their effectiveness thus far, work councils in at least some cases have obviously become an arena of struggle between contending forces.

As in the case of managerial elections, the larger significance of work councils in the late 1980s was to be found not primarily in their immediate impact on the distribution of authority but in the vision they invoked of a possible democratization of the workplace in the not-too-distant future. Widespread discussion of work councils provided the opportunity to popularize novel ideas on how such democratization might be implemented. One illustration will suffice at this point. The authors of an article in the principal journal of the State Committee on Wages and Social Issues argued that the work councils should function as "democratic forms of coordinating the interests of different social groups" at the enterprise (Katul'skii and Kobiakov, 1988, pp. 68–69). All of these groups, including not only the principal occupational categories but women and youth as well, should have their representatives in the work councils. Such representatives would be expected to promote "the realization of the interests of their group." Moreover, whenever decisions were made affecting the interests of a particular group, its views must be taken into account, and it should even have "the right of veto." Without spelling out precisely how the diverse interests of these various groups would be coordinated or reconciled, it seemed obvious to Katul'skii and Kobiakov that enterprise directors should not normally serve as chairmen of work councils. After all, it made little sense to have a functionary (*dolzhnostnoe litso*), still "representing first of all the interests of the state," serve as the head of an "organ of self-management."

Was such a conception of work councils an idle dream or a realistic possibility under Soviet circumstances? Whatever the answer to this question, it should be noted that there was a striking similarity between this conception of the work council as a kind of representative assembly and the view expressed at about the same time by the reformist sociologist T. Zaslavskaia that democracy (not yet available "in excess") was essentially a state of affairs in which all social groups have the right to "express, defend and implement their own interests" (1989a, p. 147). Our point is that attempts to implement the 1988 State Enterprise Law, and in particular the public discussion of the problems associated with the conduct of managerial elections and the functioning of elected work councils, contributed to a larger process that might be loosely characterized as the development of a "democratic consciousness." Some additional illustrations of the emergence of such a consciousness in the context of workplace relationships are given below.

Beyond the "Electoral Model" and Other Issues

A considerable range of ideas and concepts associated with the general theme of the democratization of management (or industrial democracy) received a sympathetic hearing and thus some degree of legitimacy in the late 1980s. The ideas in question included, but went considerably beyond, those discussed immediately above (managerial elections and work councils as organs of collective decision making). The process of assimilating and explicitly defending some of these ideas and concepts that had earlier been either unfamiliar or absolutely beyond the pale may be illustrated briefly by means of the following three examples.

1. Not long after the State Enterprise Law (with its novel election provisions) went into effect, voices were heard appealing for increased reliance on "direct self-management" and a readiness to move beyond the "electoral model" (Alekseev and Maksimov, 1988). Given the extremely limited Soviet experience with anything approximating genuine elections, the suspicion naturally arises that the hidden meaning of such an appeal was an invitation to return to familiar "command" methods of decision making. Had the electoral model really become so familiar that it was already time to move beyond it? But a careful reading of the argument of the sociologists Alekseev and Maksimov suggests that they were pointing to the need to supplement and enrich this model rather than to abandon it. While the electoral model (the authors focused, in particular, on the work councils) was "a great step forward," workers' participation in collective decision making should not be restricted to the act of selecting their representatives. To expand the sphere of "direct self-management," for Alekseev and Maksimov, meant providing the opportunity for literally all members of the work group to be involved in decisions traditionally made by "officialdom." While this was obviously not appropriate for all issues, there were some where it appeared perfectly reasonable—for example, decisions bearing on the distribution of resources for the "social infrastructure." How should available funds for such purposes be divided among the construction of additional housing, new child-care facilities, or recreational facilities (say, a swimming pool)? How should available housing space be distributed among members of the work collective? These were the kinds of issues that could be decided through majority vote at general meetings of the entire work unit or with the aid of scientifically conducted public-opinion surveys ("factory referendums") that would serve as a guide to the work councils. On such issues these councils would not func-

tion primarily as decision-making bodies but would organize the discussion, present the alternatives, and implement the decisions of the work force. In short, Alekseev's and Maksimov's appeal for the extension of "direct self-management" was an attempt to legitimate what in Western circles has sometimes been characterized as participatory democracy—but in fairly restricted areas of decision making. As noted earlier, there was no implication here that representative democracy (to whatever small degree it had been attained) should be forgone, only that additional opportunities for collective decision making at the workplace should be created.

2. The emergence in the late 1980s of a broad range of "informal associations"—unregistered, unofficial clubs and organizations—is a large subject that merits separate study. However, one particular aspect of this process does concern us at this point. Some of the "official" literature[11] on labor problems explicitly welcomed the appearance of independent workers' clubs whose stated aims included the protection of the rights of working people and the "development of new forms of industrial democracy and self-management of work collectives" (Korshunova and Novosel'tsev, 1989). This variety of labor literature attributed the appearance of such clubs largely to the failure of "social organizations"—in this case the focus was on official trade unions—to respond to the legitimate grievances of Soviet workers. Moreover, Korshunova and Novosel'tsev portrayed the membership of the independent workers' clubs they studied in generally positive terms. Such members were often "leading workers" with high degrees of skill, an "active life position," and interested in implementing "real *perestroika*" at the workplace (ibid., p. 70). When asked why they could not accomplish their objectives by working in official organizations, a typical response was that the latter were "fully under the control of the bureaucratic apparatus." But now that the informal clubs were publicly calling attention to workers' grievances (the cases cited included excessive overtime, wages below the legal minimum, unjustified dismissals of worker–militants), the official organizations had become more

responsive. Thus for Korshunova and Novosel'tsev (interestingly enough, they were associated with the All-Union Central Council of Trade Unions) the activities of most unofficial workers' clubs were a healthy manifestation of "socialist pluralism." Relying on language more familiar in a Western context, we might say that such writings were an implicit argument for recognizing the positive functions of "freedom of association."

3. Like the emergence of "informal" or unofficial workers' clubs, Soviet workers' strikes in the late 1980s merit a separate study, which we do not undertake here. For our purposes the principal point to be made in this context is that at a fairly early stage in the strike movement (before the rash of miners' walkouts in the summer of 1989), a variety of publications had appeared urging the recognition of the strike weapon as a legitimate form of struggle by Soviet workers in pursuit of their own interests. For those who adopted this position, like the sociologist A.K. Nazimova, the strike was "one of the forms of the contemporary democratic process." Legal recognition of the right to strike would be a sign of "the maturity of society and the development of democracy" in the Soviet Union (Roundtable 1989b, pp. 27, 33). Whatever the economic costs of strikes, they signaled the active involvement of workers in public issues, the overcoming of the passivity and "social corrosion" that had been so costly in the past (Leont'eva, 1989, pp. 124–25). These sentiments were by no means the only ones reflected in the published commentaries on the new phenomenon of strikes. Some voices from the past continued to echo the theme that the strike was "a specific offspring of the capitalist mode of production" and was incompatible with a developed socialist society—which unfortunately the Soviet Union had not yet become. Others saw the strike as a necessary outcome of increased reliance on "commodity-money relations" and thus an argument against excessive haste in the extension of the market mechanism (Roundtable 1989b, pp. 24, 31). But the increasingly dominant view was reflected in the novel conception of the strike as "a normal manifestation of democ-

racy," with no implication that this connection was an argument against the extension of democracy (Leont'eva, 1989, p. 123).

Thus, however limited the actual democratization of workplace relationships in 1987–89, this period witnessed an explosion of ideas directed toward legitimating and popularizing various forms of collective decision making by workers. Ranging from the justification for elections of managers and workers' assemblies with decision-making authority, to the legitimacy of organized protest and membership in unofficial workers' associations, these ideas signaled the demise of a long-established managerial ideology. This process of the development of a "democratic consciousness," however, was not confined to the sphere of workplace relationships. We now examine some of its manifestations in the society at large, particularly in the political sphere.

Notes

1. For another illustration of the invocation of the primacy of "social criteria" at about the same time, see Zaslavskaia (1989a), ch. 5.

2. For some additional examples of the Soviet literature on alienation during this period, see my introduction to Zaslavskaia (1989a).

3. We are not suggesting that this was the only justification for worker participation in the view of Gordon and his colleagues. They posed the issue of democratization of the society at large before this became a common theme in the late 1980s (see, for example, Gordon and Nazimova, 1984, p. 37). But the principal justification was obviously of an economic nature.

4. For an English translation of Zaslavskaia's argument, see Zaslavskaia (1989a), pp. 72–77.

5. Veber draws on the work of Richard Freeman and James Medoff as the principal source of the findings pointing to a positive correlation between the extent of unionization and productive efficiency.

6. For another illustration of a critical attitude toward managerial elections, see V. Vashchenko (1988). For Vashchenko, real democracy has its place "outside the factory gate."

7. Gerchikov and Proshkin also specified certain situations in which it would be advisable to do without managerial elections, for example, at the initial stage of the creation of a new enterprise (before employees are sufficiently acquainted with one another) or when the employees are torn by sharp "intergroup conflicts." But these were clearly regarded as exceptional cases.

8. Similar reports indicating violations of democratic procedures may be

found in Gerchikov and Proshkin, 1988, p. 102; Shustov, 1988; Iarkho, 1988, p. 68. A generally positive assessment of the democratic nature of managerial elections in the Vladimir region may be found in Morozov (1988, p. 56).

9. Torkanovskii has reported that in 1989 "more than 20 percent of directors of enterprises and 6–8 percent of foremen and shop chiefs were elected on a competitive basis" (Torkanovskii, 1990, p. 103).

10. "The administration basically took into its own hands the creation of councils of the work collective and led them. Using its commanding position, it appropriated to itself the right to decide everything in the name of the collective and for it" (Puginskii, 1989, p. 33).

11. Our principal source here is an article by two sociologists associated with the All-Union Central Council of Trade Unions, which appeared in the principal organ of the State Committee on Labor and Social Issues (Korshunova and Novosel'tsev). Hence our characterization of it as part of the "official" literature.

3

The Democratization of Political Discourse

When the concept of "democratization" was invoked in Soviet discussions during the early Gorbachev years (1985–87), the usual context was economic decision making and plant management. Thus democratization was largely identified with providing increased opportunity for enterprise autonomy and initiative and for worker participation in plant-level managerial decisions. This was reflected in a typical formulation in the literature on the need for "radical renewal" early in 1987: "The CPSU attaches paramount importance to the development of democracy in the sphere of production" (*Rabochii klass*, 1987, p. 8). The reforms projected and discussed in those years were essentially economic reforms, and democratization (in the sense indicated above) was one aspect of this anticipated reform process. The initial version of the State Enterprise Law issued at the beginning of 1987 (with its provisions for elections of managers and work councils), and most of the commentary that immediately followed, seemed to reinforce this association of democratization with enterprise autonomy and collective decision making at the workplace.

By the end of 1987, however, Soviet discussions in this area had begun to move well beyond the simple identification of democratization with proposed changes "in the sphere of production." In the language that was to be increasingly invoked to characterize the forthcoming reform process, "radical restructuring" was recognized as necessary in the political sphere no less than in the economic (Migranian, 1987, p. 91). Sounding a theme that would often be repeated in the closing years of the decade, A.G. Zdravomyslov called for "democratization of the entire system of social relationships" in the Soviet Union (1987, p. 6). For some participants in these discussions, the extension of democratization to the political sphere—whatever its other justifications—was a necessary condition for the kind of economic reform that would increase the decision-making power of enterprise management and enhance worker participation in that management. Economic decentralization and the democratization of management could hardly be taken seriously in the absence of a more democratic environment in the society at large (Rakitskaia and Rakitskii, 1988; Gerchikov, 1989).

But the strictly economic justification for political democratization encompassed only part of a wide range of ideas that received a public hearing in the late 1980s. However one assesses the extent of changes in Soviet political institutions during these years, it is surely the case that the democratization of political discourse took a giant step forward in this period. New concepts were introduced, old ones abandoned, and unprecedented controversies raged on the appropriate pace and limits of democratization. These are our principal concerns in this chapter. Unlike our approach in chapter 2, where we examined the new legal and institutional framework associated with workplace democratization, our focus here is almost exclusively on the ideas that emerged in Soviet discussions of political democratization. These ideas and the controversies they generated obviously contributed to—but were also a response to—institutional changes in Soviet political life: the emergence of "informal" political clubs, multiple-candidate elections for the Congress of People's Deputies, and the legislative activities of the new Soviet parliament. Put more succinctly, we examine the initial stages of a process that may be characterized as the propagation of democratic values in the Soviet Union of the late 1980s.

In Defense of a Socialist "Civil Society"

Although very much a part of the Marxian ideological heritage, the concept of civil society has only recently been assimilated into the Soviet political and philosophical literature. In 1987–89 it became an integral part of the new language of democratization, confronting readers of both "academic" journals and daily newspapers. The writings of A.M. Migranian in those years were among the first to elaborate the concept of civil society and demonstrate its relevance to the issue of reforming the Soviet political system (1987, 1988a).

Migranian's exposition of the concept highlighted the striking contrast between what he characterized as the Marxian vision of the new socialist society and Soviet reality. "Does the state always and everywhere absorb society and the individual? Is this what we wanted in making our revolution?" (1988a, p. 1). Acknowledging that early Marxist writings had used the concept of civil society in a variety of ways, Migranian identified its underlying common element as the sphere of "nonpolitical" or "nonstate" relations. It was in this sphere, particularly in the realm of economic relations ("basic relations between antagonistic classes" in Migranian's formulation), that Marxian theory expected the social revolution would have its decisive impact. The supplanting of private property and the domination of the former ruling classes would signal the "emancipation" or "unshackling" of civil society. That is, the "nonantagonistic classes" constituting the new society would gain control of the means of production, thereby setting the stage for ultimately dispensing with the state as an organ that historically reinforced the domination of exploiting classes over the exploited in civil society. Migranian made a point of stressing that in the original Marxian vision the transition to socialism would mark the beginning of "a process of contraction of the political sphere, the sphere of state regulation," and a steady enhancement of the role of civil society. More specifically, this meant that (pending the extinction of the state and the ultimate attainment of a somewhat nebulous condition of "communist self-government") individuals organized in "a variety of voluntary civic organizations and associations" (including cooperatives, labor collectives, trade unions, "creative unions") would have increasing opportunity to affect political decision making. Moreover, even after the adoption of political decisions, normally "by majority vote," those favoring the minority position would have the right to continue bringing their counterarguments to public notice. This was a "necessary condition for the normal functioning of a socialist society" (1987, p. 77).

Our concern here is not with the feasibility of this conception of a socialist transition, or whether Migranian's version of what he calls "Marxian political theory" offers a reasonably accurate portrait of the original. The point is rather that the anticipated socialist society sketched by Migranian, particularly with respect to relations between the state and civil society, was so utterly at odds with the system that actually emerged. What went wrong, and how could the damage begin to be undone? The response of Migranian, as well as the writings of others who implicitly confronted this question by stressing the need for the reemergence of a civil society, had obvious implications for both political and economic reform.

Migranian's response to this question went approximately as follows. Given the underdeveloped economy bequeathed to the revolutionaries by the old regime (since they seized power before the old system had attained its full potential), the low cultural and educational level of the population, and the need to defend the revolution against both external and internal enemies, it is hardly surprising that centralized state power (including its "repressive organs") played such a decisive role in the immediate post-revolutionary period. In effect, the new socialist state took on functions not anticipated in Migranian's version of "the political theory of Marxism" (ibid., p. 79). In this situation, in addition to its tasks of economic and cultural "construction," the state should have assumed responsibility for encouraging the emergence of a new civil society—especially since the remnants of the old were compromised by virtue of their ties to the old system (1988a, p. 4).

That is, the state should have fostered the development of new, presumably independent "voluntary associations, unions, and organizations" whose increased involvement in the life of postrevolutionary society would have gradually replaced the "paternalistic function" and "tutelage" of state authorities. Of course what transpired was the very opposite of this hoped-for process. Following the brief respite of the New Economic Policy, the "total regulation of all spheres of the life of society" associated with collectivization and the industrialization process meant that the "nonpolitical" or nonstate sphere of society was "reduced practically to zero." In effect the state absorbed civil society, leaving no room for unofficial ("spontaneous and unsanctioned" in Migranian's formulation) activity by either individuals or social groups.

Thus, when Migranian then appeals for the "institutionalization of civil society" as defining the political content of *perestroika*, he is calling for an institutional mechanism that would permit citizens grouped in various "voluntary associations" to exercise effective influence on (and eventually "full control over") the organs of state power. But at least in his early writings on these matters (1987, p. 82), Migranian frankly recognized that there were clear limitations on the types of organizations that could participate in this process of democratization. Thus while acknowledging the need for all citizens to be able to "freely express their judgments" on current issues and for a genuine legislature that would exercise control over the executive branch of government, he explicitly denied that the process of achieving "consensus through conflict" that would follow the reemergence of an independent civil society required "competing political parties."

Before long, however, such qualifications began to disappear from the literature popularizing the concept of civil society. Indeed, as the discussion progressed in 1988–90, we may observe a steady "escalation" in the institutional changes cited in the literature as necessarily accompanying the assimilation of a civil society. In 1988, in the course of welcoming the appearance of independent "informal groups," E. Ambartsumov looked forward to the emergence of a socialist civil society that would function as a "counterweight" to the state (Roundtable, 1988a, p. 8). Such a counterweight was surely needed given the long-standing "monopoly of the center over political initiative." Like any monopoly, noted Ambartsumov, this contributed to "decay" and was responsible for widespread political "passivity." Thus Ambartsumov's exposition of the civil society concept was essentially linked to the need for the "destatization of society." But in the course of this exposition he also invoked the need to transform the political sphere into an arena in which different "social interests" would openly confront one another, in which multiple-candidate elections would become the norm, and in which society would ultimately assert its control not only over the state but also "over the party" (Ambartsumov, 1988). These formulations, particularly the last point, obviously extended the implications of a civil society beyond the limits accepted in Migranian's pioneering work. But subsequent discussions went even further.

The issue that began to be raised with increasing frequency concerned the economic foundations of a civil society. Thus for A. Butenko (1989d) such a society (essentially a "system of associations of independent citizens") must provide its citizens with the opportunity to exercise "personal economic independence." More specifically, this meant that citizens must have the right to choose among alternative sources of employment rooted in diverse forms of property ownership, ranging from (decentralized) state and cooperative property to "family and individual property." For another participant in these discussions (Ionin, 1990), the market mechanism was one of the "pillars" of a civil society (along with a law-based state and political freedom). "But is a market possible without private property?" The writer who posed the question did not undertake an answer, suggesting that the issue remained unresolved. But for others the issue already seemed closed. Private property serves as a necessary "material foundation" for a civil society (Seliunin, 1989, p. 212).

Writing in 1988, Ambartsumov seemed concerned with the

changes required to create a "socialist" civil society. The more recent literature on the concept tends to omit the adjective.

Reassessing "Bourgeois Democracy"

Given the positive connotation associated with the concept of civil society in the recent Soviet literature (more specifically, the notion of the "primacy" of civil society over the state), it should come as no surprise that long-standing Soviet assessments of "bourgeois democracy" (essentially, modern capitalist political institutions) have undergone significant modification. The kind of crude, one-dimensional characterizations of Western political systems that were common in earlier years may be illustrated by the following relatively restrained commentary published in the late 1970s:

> As long as the basic foundation of the capitalist mode of production—private property in the means of production and the exploitation of hired labor—remains inviolable, bourgeois democracy will be the same as Lenin characterized it, i.e., a restricted, partial democracy for the rich against the poor. The adaptation and modernization of bourgeois political institutions under conditions of the scientific-technical revolution does not change their class nature, their oppressive character, and does not make them more democratic. (Kerimov, 1976, pp. 104–5)

These traditional formulations, commonly supplemented by the summary proposition that capitalist political institutions invariably function as the open or disguised dictatorship of the ruling class, are precisely the kind that by the late 1980s would be characterized as representing "primitive and stereotypical conceptions of bourgeois democracy" (Roundtable, 1988b, p. 15). The new approach that emerged in those years did not signify an uncritically positive assessment of Western democracy, but it clearly signaled a marked departure from the sentiments cited above. Put simply, the emphasis in Soviet discussions shifted to "assimilating" some elements of Western political institutions rather than "exposing" their limitations. The justification for the new approach was obvious. If the prospects for democratization of the Soviet system were to be taken seriously, it was necessary to draw on "the whole of the world-historical experience of the struggle for democracy," obviously including the achievements of what had previously been contemptuously dismissed as bourgeois democracy (ibid., pp. 5–6) While the latter typically functioned in a manner that perpetuated capitalist class domination, it also incorporated basic principles whose significance transcended the particular system (capitalism) in which they were embodied. S. Peregudov, one of the participants in these discussions, illustrated the point by invoking the basic principle of "political representation" itself, whose principal elements he characterized as "parties, elections, representative institutions, the primacy of the latter over all other political institutions" (ibid., p. 8). Although obviously associated with bourgeois democracy, these principles and procedures were no less desirable and necessary under socialism. Just look, noted Peregudov, at the "negative consequences" stemming from their absence—whether under capitalism or socialism.

Other discussants pointed to the apparent link between the core political and economic institutions of developed capitalist societies. Indeed, for K. Kholodkovskii there seemed to be a "complete analogy" between bourgeois political democracy with its principle of "juridical equality of individuals," competitive elections, and parliamentary pluralism on the one hand, and "market principles" of capitalist economic organization on the other (ibid., pp. 12–13). Moreover, Kholodkovskii's invocation of this "analogy" was not presented in a manner suggesting a negative assessment of either the "market principles" or the corresponding political practices. Indeed, the opposite was the case.

The reassessment of Western political institutions was also reflected in the readiness of the Soviet literature to acknowledge the process of "enrichment" undergone by bourgeois democracy since the early nineteenth century. Thus (according to Kholodkovskii) only the "most radical democrats" of that period could have dreamed that the "boundaries of political democracy" (in modern capitalist societies) would have expanded to include uni-

versal suffrage, regional and local self-government, and enhanced economic and political rights of trade unions. Particularly
welcome for Peregudov were signs of increased opportunities for
the implementation of "direct," or "functional," democracy, a
process reflected most recently in the enhanced influence of the
ecology movement and consumer-protection organizations and
somewhat earlier in the increased role of trade unions in management and economic policy-making (ibid., pp. 13–14).

Perhaps the most challenging formulation of the significance
of the expanding limits of "bourgeois democracy" was suggested
by Migranian. The process of democratization of political life in
the more developed capitalist countries had so transformed these
societies that the very concept of "bourgeois democracy" (implying the domination of the political process by a particular class)
was now called into question. The concept was perfectly appropriate, in Migranian's view, when applied to the nineteenth century. But it hardly seemed appropriate under conditions in which
working-class parties, by virtue of electoral victories, could attain
political power (as they had in a number of European countries)
and use existing political institutions "to implement social transformations in the interests of those whom they represented." Was
it not absurd to characterize as "bourgeois" a system that permitted such a high degree of "free play of political forces"?
Migranian's point was rejected by the leader of the roundtable
discussion we have reviewed here, G. Diligenskii (ibid., pp. 16–
18), but the very nature of the latter's criticism of the former
suggested the changing tone of Soviet discussions in this area
and the concepts on which they have come to rely. Surely, noted
Diligenskii, economic power in civil society continued to rest predominantly in the hands of the bourgeoisie, and since civil society
retained its "primacy" over the state (a point stressed by Migranian
himself), the political inequality or disparity (*neravnopravie*) between the bourgeoisie and the working class in capitalist societies remained a "fact." In this sense, argued Diligenskii, the
concept of "bourgeois democracy"—implying some limitation on
democracy—retained its relevance. But there was nothing about

this qualified reaffirmation of an old concept that could be interpreted as denying the evidence of "enrichment" of Western political institutions cited by the other participants in this discussion.

The more sympathetic treatment of Western political institutions in the Soviet political literature was also apparent in the manner in which socialist democracy was distinguished from its bourgeois predecessor. Even the manner of posing the question signaled a new approach: When Diligenskii asked the participants in this discussion how they saw the essential difference between Western democracy and socialist democracy he made it clear that the latter referred not to any existing state of affairs but to the kind of system that would eventually emerge from the process of "democratization" currently under way. Those who directly confronted the question stressed that the future socialist democracy would seek to correct the "imbalance" (presumably common in capitalist democracies) between "representative and direct systems of political participation" by substantially expanding opportunities for direct popular participation in decision making "at all levels of public life" (Roundtable, 1989a, pp. 83–84). But there was nothing about such a response that detracted from the importance of first assimilating those representative forms of participation that Western political systems had already established. Perhaps the most explicit recognition of this point in the Soviet political literature appeared in an article by A. Buzgalin as the decade of the eighties drew to a close (1989, p. 35): "In my view, political liberation presupposes as a minimum the full implementation of all bourgeois-democratic freedoms (the election and removability of the higher state apparatus, and freedom of speech, conscience, association, unions, etc.)." Clearly, the more serious Soviet literature on "bourgeois democracy" in this period made its contribution to the propagation of democratic values.[1]

Studying Public Opinion

As the 1980s drew to a close, among the items that began to appear with increasing frequency in Soviet publications were reports of public opinion surveys. Such surveys had been conducted earlier, of course, but 1988–89 witnessed an unprecedented expansion in the range of issues on which respondents were questioned, an obvious improvement in the quality of the resources invested in these surveys, and a readiness to publicize findings that were on occasion politically sensitive in nature. Among the principal organizations conducting these surveys were the All-Union Center for the Study of Public Opinion headed by Academician T. Zaslavskaia and the Institute of Sociology under the directorship of V. Iadov. Samples of Soviet citizens were asked to give their reactions to the following issues, among others: the operations of the "parliament" (the Congress of People's Deputies), attitudes toward particular members of this body, expectations (or lack of such) associated with *perestroika*, the desirability of managerial elections, the relative urgency of different economic problems, the proposed expansion of cooperatives and leasing arrangements, the desirability of a multiparty system and elections to choose the country's head of state, the desirability of extending private property and (privately) hired labor.

Our chief purpose here is not to review the findings of these public opinion surveys (although a word will be said about some of them below) or to assess their validity. These are matters for a separate project. Our interest for the moment lies elsewhere. How was the conduct of such surveys and the popularization of their findings justified—both to state and party authorities (who presumably had to approve them) and to the reading public at large? Given the range and sensitivity of some of the issues raised and the sheer explosion in the volume of such surveys, how did the principal organizers of these studies defend the legitimacy of their novel absorption in the study of public opinion? The reason for posing the question should be obvious. The answer to it illustrates another channel through which some Soviet intellectuals sought to promote the growth of a "democratic consciousness." This becomes apparent from a brief examination of the responses to the above question implicit in the writings of B.A. Grushin, Zaslavskaia, and Iadov.

Grushin's elaboration of the concept of the "normal function-ing" of public opinion probably comes as close to a civil libertar-ian position as anything ever published in the Soviet Union. Grushin identified two necessary conditions for such "normal functioning." The first, quite simply, was that public opinion must have the opportunity to "speak out publicly, freely, and fully on all questions that concern it." As if to dispel any doubt about his meaning, Grushin made it clear that this applied to the "full spectrum" of opinions in society. A socialist democracy must permit the expression of "any opinion on any question" (Grushin, 1988, pp. 27–28). But the second condition for the normal operation of public opinion was no less important. This involved creating the conditions that would guarantee reliance on public opinion in the "mechanisms of power," in decision mak-ing on major public issues. In other words, freedom of expression must be supplemented by public opinion functioning as a "politi-cal institution" (1989, p. 3). While these were rather general formulations, they were also Grushin's principal arguments for increased reliance on professionally conducted public opinion surveys.

The case for such polls was made in essentially similar terms by Zaslavskaia and Iadov, but some of their arguments also had a rather more pragmatic—some might say technocratic—quality. For Zaslavskaia (1989c) the effective functioning of the new So-viet parliament required that it have at its disposal reliable infor-mation on the population's attitudes concerning issues under consideration for legislative action. How did different sectors of the population assess the relative urgency of various economic and social problems? What was their reaction to reformist mea-sures already adopted? Both for Iadov (1989) and for Zaslavskaia (1989b) the "voice of the people"—as elicited in professionally conducted public opinion surveys—could serve as a reliable feedback mechanism guiding "optimal" policy-making decisions by state authorities and alerting them to the emergence of new grievances and possible sources of group conflict.

But there was another function that studies of public opinion could perform that seemed equally important, if not more so, for these sociologists. It involved the positive impact that the conduct of such studies and the practice of publicizing their results could be expected to have on the citizenry itself. People would become increasingly accustomed to the idea that it is perfectly natural for public opinion to be "pluralistic, mosaic-like, containing points of view that do not agree or are even directly opposed" (in Iadov's formulation). The resulting atmosphere would encourage a sense of engagement in dialogue. Zaslavskaia (1989b) invoked the metaphor of public opinion polls functioning as society's "mirror," which not only made it possible for people to "see" themselves but also encouraged them "to listen to the arguments of others." Iadov made essentially the same point when he suggested that people confronting the results of such polls would become increasingly aware that achieving consensus and solving problems requires that "one must take into account not only one's own but also other points of view, and be able and ready to compromise."

Were such expectations reasonable in the Soviet context, or did these arguments serve mainly as affirmations of their proponents' own democratic values? Any attempt to assess the full impact of Soviet public opinion surveys would be inappropriate at this point. But it does seem clear that at least some of these surveys, and the particular manner in which their results were presented, contributed to an intellectual environment in which "the arguments of others" were increasingly seen as legitimate elements of normal political discourse. Moreover, the "others" in question sometimes included those whose views were at odds with the very core of traditional Soviet ideology. Nowhere is this more clearly illustrated than in those surveys of public opinion that asked samples of Soviet citizens whether they favored the introduction of a multiparty system (Amelin, 1989) and the extension of privately owned means of production (Shpil'ko, 1989). The simple fact that sampled respondents were confronted with alternative ways of answering such questions itself constituted an implicit "argument"—an assertion of the legitimacy of disagreement on formerly sacred truths. The argument was reinforced by the manner in which the results were presented. There was nothing in the published summaries of these results to suggest that the sizable minorities of respondents who favored a multiparty system (40 percent of the intelligentsia sample and almost a quarter of local party functionaries) and the legal operation of "large private enterprises" (one-fourth of the sample) represented a less enlightened sector of the population than the majorities who opposed them.[2] The positive functions attributed by Zaslavskaia and Iadov to studies of public opinion certainly seemed applicable in these cases. Perhaps the chief contribution of such studies is that they tended to dissolve the former distinction between "official" or sanctioned views and nonofficial views. In effect, almost any view on a particular issue could now be regarded as sanctioned or at least deserving of a hearing. The particular studies just described seemed to embody Grushin's principle of "any opinion on any question."

We now turn to the substance of some controversies on political issues, particularly on the process of democratization, that emerged in the late 1980s.

On the Transition to Democracy

A principal feature of Soviet political discussions in this period is that they were at least as much absorbed with the nature of the transition to democracy as with the detailed functioning of a future democratic political system. Thus the model building that one finds in the political literature is no less—perhaps more—concerned with the "democratization" process than with the end product of this process. This is hardly surprising given the turmoil and uncertainty associated with the projected reform of a political system that had been essentially frozen for decades. But this focus on the transition process also reflected the decidedly provocative views on this matter of some Soviet political scientists and the readiness of others to challenge them.

Once again the spark was provided by some ideas developed

by A.M. Migranian. At a time when serious discussions of political reform had barely begun, and before any significant institutional changes had been introduced, Migranian called attention to a "universal law" allegedly derived by Tocqueville ("one of the greatest political thinkers of modern times") and applicable to countries on the threshold of "modernization and democratization." In Migranian's formulation the law could be stated very simply and directly: For countries without a democratic tradition, "there is nothing more dangerous than excessively rapid reforms and changes." Excessive haste in the democratization process could lead to the reimposition of a brutal tyranny (Migranian, 1988b, p. 109). Migranian's invocation of Tocqueville's warning was obviously linked to his own conception of certain necessary features of a successful transition to democracy under Soviet circumstances.

The point of departure of Migranian's approach was the apparent absence of any historical precedents for a direct transition (peacefully, by reform "from above") from a totalitarian political system to a democratic one. But there was abundant evidence of the transformation of authoritarian regimes into democratic political systems. Both recent history (Migranian pointed to the cases of Franco's Spain, Portugal, and Greece) as well as the earlier transition to democratic political systems in Western Europe suggested to Migranian that without a "more or less prolonged" intervening period of authoritarian rule a successful transition from totalitarianism to democracy would be impossible in the Soviet Union. This argument was not derived simply from Migranian's reading of the historical record but rested also on his conception of the inner logic and structure of the transition process itself:

> The transition from a "classical" totalitarian system to a democracy cannot be accomplished instantly, in a single leap. As intellectual life and the economy are freed of state control, and as various forms of (nonstate) property make their appearance, society assumes greater complexity, resulting in the rapid rise of numerous and conflicting interests. The polarization of these interests and the conflict among

> them increase the danger of chaos and a collapse of the political system at the stage of radical restructuring. Therefore, while the highly complex process of forming, shaping, and establishing a civil society is in progress, it is extremely important that a firm authoritarian regime be maintained in the political sphere, a regime that would permit limited democracy at that stage. (1989a, p. 169)

In this conception, Soviet democratization, if it was to succeed, had to be seen as a process requiring careful guidance from the top. It certainly could not be left to the uncontrolled whims of mass movements. Those who sought to guide the process would have to recognize ("all of world history shows") that only a distinct sequence of changes in the various social spheres—intellectual, economic, and political—could lead to a democratic system. Writing in 1989, Migranian noted that the first stage in this "modernization" process, the freeing of intellectual life from strict state control, had already been substantially accomplished. But the second, a comparable "destatization" of economic life, had barely begun. This would require the transformation of state property into various forms of public and cooperative property and the freeing of the economic sphere from micromanagement and regimentation by the state. "Only then," with the resulting emergence of a civil society independent of the state, could one expect any substantial movement toward controlled democratization in the political sphere.

Thus Migranian's approach to the theme of democratization not only stressed the distinct stages described above but also insisted on the need to adhere to a particular sequence of reform, with the political sphere the last to be affected. This approach was reflected in his characterization of the process as necessarily "nonsynchronous" (*asinkhronnyi*) in nature. A supporter of Migranian's general position, I. Kliamkin, made essentially the same point in the form of a rather bold (excessively bold?) historical generalization. The transition from a premarket to a market economy had "never and nowhere been implemented in parallel with democratization" (Kliamkin and Migranian, 1989). Once again the implications for current Soviet policy were more than obvious. Any substantial democratization of the political system would have to follow an extended period of "destatization" of the economy. The latter process, at least initially, required the retention of an authoritarian regime. That would permit—in Migranian's words—only "limited democracy."

The principal justification for such a transitional period of authoritarian rule was clear. Migranian feared that the necessary "destatization" of the economy and the emerging civil society that would accompany it might lead to the kinds of unrestrained conflicts of group interests that could threaten political stability and thus the reform process itself. But what was the institutional content of the proposed authoritarian transition, and what would make it truly transitional rather than durable? Migranian's argument confronted both issues, the first more directly than the second. Authoritarian rule was not to be the equivalent of the "total regimentation" associated with the familiar totalitarian model. Like other authoritarian regimes, there was no reason why the Soviet version could not incorporate "certain democratic elements"—elections, a legal opposition, dissent—but all within "permissible limits" established by the authoritarian regime. The latter's principal function would be "to ensure that conflicts of interest in the society are resolved through legal procedures" and that such procedures become fully integrated into the society's political culture. As might be expected, the party's role in this process would be critical. It would be expected to function as "the supreme and ultimate arbiter in the political system," a guarantor of stability in the midst of the reform process. But—and this point needs stressing—these party functions would last no longer than the period of transition to a democratic political system. That transition, in Migranian's view, required the creation of new "independent" legislative and executive government bodies. Initially these bodies would translate party policy into legislative form and see that it was enforced. But such a transition process also required that the party steadily "distance itself" from these bodies—now representing the "institutionalized interests of civil society"—so that they could acquire genuine independence and experience in decision making on public issues. Migranian did not indicate why the former "ultimate arbiter" (the party) would readily agree to make way for independent legislative and executive authorities. However, he did project a vision of a Soviet political system that no longer required a "paternalistic" role for the party, a system in which "the separation of the state from the party, and of civil society from the state" had been attained (Roundtable, 1989a; Migranian, 1989a; 1989b). But like some other visions of the future formerly popularized in the Soviet literature, this was regarded by Migranian as applicable to a rather distant future.

There was no shortage of critical responses to Migranian's position.[3] We briefly examine some of the more substantial of these below. Perhaps the principal message of the critics was that Migranian underestimated the readiness of Soviet society and its population for political democracy.

A special target of the critics was Migranian's apparent reliance on historically prescribed patterns and sequences as reliable guides to the democratization process in the Soviet Union. For G. Diligenskii, "democracy cannot develop according to a rigid plan drawn up by political scientists." Democratization processes, by their very nature, were "highly variable" (*mnogovariantnyi*). While Migranian, in warning against excessive haste in democratizing the political sphere, had repeatedly cited the prolonged nature of the transition to bourgeois democracy in some Western societies, Diligenskii asked why must "social and political processes in the late twentieth century proceed at the same rate as in the eighteenth and nineteenth centuries?" (1989, pp. 27, 29; Roundtable, 1989a). Another critic, L. Batkin, warned against excessive reliance on historical "laws" (including those allegedly requiring that "destatization" of the economy precede democratization in the political sphere), when in fact the historical process was constantly undergoing "unforeseen readjustments." After all, such readjustments explained why Marx could not extrapolate the future of capitalism from the capitalism of his own day. Similarly, Batkin seemed to imply, Migranian's overly deterministic orientation to the necessarily prolonged nature of the democratization process was rooted in the past, not in an already transformed present. In the current "revolutionary" situation, "the population is learning in months what would ordinarily require decades" (Batkin, 1989).

There was clearly a paradoxical quality in Migranian's thought. The desired end was political democracy, the subordination of the state to freely organized civil society. Even his serious critics did not question his commitment to this goal. But its attainment, in his view, required the deliberately calculated policies of an "enlightened authoritarianism," certainly not the uncontrolled activity of self-organized democratic mass movements. There clearly was some justification for Diligenskii's charge that Migranian distrusted the masses. "When the masses become involved in the solution of serious questions, they often solve them to their own disadvantage, driven more by populist sentiments than by serious ideas" (Kliamkin and Migranian, 1989). In contrast to Migranian, Diligenskii welcomed the emergence of the new independent "informal" organizations, grassroots protest movements, and even strike committees. These were the "sprouts of genuine democracy and civil society" (1989, p. 29). While Migranian feared the potentially destabilizing impact of such movements, for Diligenskii a certain amount of destabilization was a necessary, indeed healthy, accompaniment of the democratization process.

There was one issue on which Migranian and his principal critics seemed to agree. The implementation of *perestroika*, particularly the urgently needed economic reforms (presumably the "destatization" frequently invoked in these discussions) required action by a "strong authority" (*sil'naia vlast'*). Batkin made it clear that he regarded this as "absolutely correct" and then posed a critical question: "But why cannot a democratic authority be strong?" (Batkin, 1989). The question was hardly an argument, but it was certainly a challenge. It challenged Migranian's implicit assumption that an authoritarian regime would necessarily be "stronger" than any conceivable democratic one under current circumstances and thus better able to implement required reforms in both the economic and political spheres. Given the nature of the impending reforms, however, the assumption needed challenging. After all, "destatization" of the economy implied increased enterprise autonomy, transformation of state property into various forms of cooperative and public property, and the extension of the market mechanism. Could the state *apparat* associated with the prevailing regime—surely not yet a democratic one—be expected to invoke "strong authority" to implement the kind of economic reforms that threatened to make portions of it superfluous? In other words, would not a more democratic regime rooted in support "from below" be in a stronger position to implement economic reforms? Thus Batkin's question was an implicit challenge directed at the very core of Migranian's thesis—the need for an extended authoritarian transition to democracy.

There is no way of directly gauging the impact of these discussions on public consciousness. But it seems likely that the reasoned public debate on political issues reviewed here contributed to the process that was at the center of these discussions—democratization.

The Expanding Limits of Pluralism

Soviet discussions of the conception of pluralism that emerged in 1988–89 are of interest on at least two counts. First, they illustrate the remarkable rapidity with which political views once regarded as completely at odds with the regime's dominant ideology could become legitimized and widely accepted. No less important, they also reveal a considerable diversity of views on the particular kinds of pluralism that would be appropriate in Soviet society. It will become apparent below that the range of differences in Soviet attitudes toward political pluralism cannot be neatly reduced to a simple and unambiguous dichotomy of "conservative" and "liberal" views. There are significant gradations within these categories as well. The following discussion distinguishes four Soviet responses to the issue of pluralism.

1. One such response, clearly conservative in nature, may be characterized as the minimalist version of pluralism. When the need to affirm the legitimacy of a "socialist pluralism of opinions" became part of Soviet public discourse in 1987–88, the principal concern of some discussants became that of restricting the limits of a legitimate pluralism. The absorption with spelling out these limits, with specifying what should remain unchanged, is the distinguishing feature of the minimalist version. Some of the views expressed at a roundtable discussion of pluralism organized by the principal Soviet sociological journal in 1988 provide clear illustrations. Thus, for one of the participants, V.N. Ivanov, while "clashes of opinion" and "opposing points of view" were perfectly normal under conditions of *perestroika*, there was no place for a pluralism of basic ideologies. "If by this we mean the development of some ideology alternative to Marxist-Leninist and socialist ideology, it seems to me that there is no real basis for this, no real meaning to this" (Roundtable, 1988c, p. 8). As might be expected, adherents of the minimalist version of pluralism explicitly rejected the notion of a multiparty system. Even some who appealed for an extension of "intellectual pluralism" and for recognizing the legitimacy of "pluralism in the political sphere" felt compelled to add that these objectives were perfectly compatible with the retention of the prevailing one-party system. Some of the more inflexible adherents of minimalist pluralism also refused to recognize the newly emerging unofficial "informal groups" as legitimate manifestations of socialist pluralism. What was needed was a "healthy pluralism" within the party, not a multiplicity of independent community and political groups outside it (ibid., pp. 9, 13, 15; Vasil'ev, 1989, p. 101).

Although the above position was a common one, at least in the initial stages of Soviet discussions of pluralism, it is not easy to find in the political literature of this period anything approximating a full-fledged and elaborate defense of the one-party system. Justifications were offered, of course, but they were more in the nature of brief and familiar pronouncements than of extended logical or empirical arguments. Thus, for G. Merkurov (1988, p. 61) the one-party system was so deeply rooted in prevailing political structures and traditions that a move away from it would necessarily be destabilizing ("the minuses would greatly outweigh the plusses").[4] For another defender of the existing political system, P.N. Fedoseev (1989, pp. 17–18), there was no reason why the one existing party could not express and "reconcile" the vital interests of "all strata of society, all its social and national groups." The absence of basic "class antagonisms" and conflicting class interests (such as those prevailing in capitalist societies) presumably made a multiplicity of parties unnecessary.

By 1989 some adherents of the minimalist version could invoke a new phenomenon in Soviet society to justify their view that meaningful "socialist pluralism" was possible within the framework of a one-party system—the proceedings of the Congress of People's Deputies (ibid., p. 15; Vasil'ev, 1989, p. 101). But at about the same time, some of the more flexible spokesmen for minimalist pluralism seemed ready to abandon their insistence on a one-party system—with strict qualifications, however. Thus, R.I. Kosolapov, who in 1988 argued that given a "healthy pluralism" within the single ruling party, "everything else would follow," by 1989 was prepared to contemplate the possibility of a dual-party system. The simple qualification added by Kosolapov was that both parties accept a "Marxist-Leninist platform" (compare Roundtable, 1988c, p. 15, and Roundtable, 1989c, pp. 59–60). It hardly seems necessary to add that such a position did not qualify as a departure from a minimalist version of political pluralism (although Kosolapov saw the result as essentially comparable to the United States model in which the two parties implement "if not identical, then generally similar policies").

Given the intellectual ferment of the late 1980s, one cannot help but wonder whether the quality of the arguments of some defenders of minimalist pluralism had an effect that was directly the opposite of that intended.

2. Another response to the issue of pluralism, that of A.M. Migranian (whose views were at the center of much of Soviet

political debate during this period), bears a surface similarity to the position of the minimalists described above. The differences, however, seem more important than any similarities. Migranian sought to demonstrate that pluralism in the political sphere (institutional arrangements assuring "opportunities for political expression by the diverse social, professional, and other interests in society") could be implemented through mechanisms other than a multiparty system. But unlike the minimalist version, Migranian's argument was not linked to the restrictive notion of pluralism within a single party, at least not in the long run. Indeed, what he projected may be characterized as a vision of pluralism outside the party system—whether of a one-party or multiparty type. Such a course would parallel recent developments in the West, where, in Migranian's view, the principal instruments of pluralism had become a variety of "interest groups," sometimes operating within political parties but with increasing frequency independently of them (1988b, pp. 117–21). If a reformed Soviet political system was to be guided by Western experience, this was the process that had to be assimilated.

As suggested earlier, for Migranian the critical condition required for the development of pluralism was the "institutionalization of civil society." This was a state of affairs that could only be attained as a result of the "destatization" of economic, social, and cultural life followed by the creation of "independent and self-governing" organizations in these and other spheres of public life. These organizations would function as "interest groups" (roughly comparable to those in Western societies), seeking support for candidates to legislative and executive bodies that would best articulate and defend their interests "in the sphere of political decision making" (ibid., p. 120). It seemed perfectly natural to Migranian that in the period of transition to the new system the familiar ruling party would function as "arbiter and conciliator" of conflicting group interests. But this function of the party, and indeed the party itself, would become superfluous once the institutions of civil society (now represented in the legislative and executive branches of government) became involved in "the process of civilized democratic resolution of conflicts in the political sphere" (Roundtable, 1989a, p. 81). The somewhat idealized and imprecise formulations on which Migranian relied should not obscure the essential vision he projected. It was one in which "society itself," acting not through a vanguard party but through the independent and pluralistic (albeit nonparty) structures of an emancipated civil society, would formulate its own goals in the political arena and the policies required to meet them.[5]

Whatever its limitations, such a vision was clearly a significant step beyond the minimalist version of pluralism discussed above. But Migranian left no room for, or at the very least ignored, a critical component of any meaningful concept of political pluralism—the notion of a political opposition.

3. In the initial stages of Soviet discussions of pluralism, support for a multiparty system (or something very close to it) was typically expressed in somewhat indirect terms, but the intended meaning was surely apparent. What else could S. Tolstikov have meant early in 1988 when he appealed for creating opportunities "to express alternative political initiatives both in the party itself . . . as well as in the whole sphere of sociopolitical life" (Roundtable, 1988a, p. 11)? Before long, however, such circumlocutions would become unnecessary. By the end of 1988 *Izvestiia* carried an article affirming that a multiparty system should be regarded as a normal feature of a "full-scale socialist democracy" (Kurashvili, 1988b), and in the months that followed, arguments in defense of such a system (some of which will be examined below) could readily be found in Soviet publications.

In retrospect, it seems perfectly natural that the issue of multiparty politics eventually moved to the forefront of Soviet discussions of pluralism. If there was ever a theme in Soviet political discourse that lent itself to an expansionary logic, it was the theme of pluralism. At all stages of these discussions we may observe two conflicting currents: the efforts of some to confine pluralism to the narrowest possible limits, and the efforts of others constantly to transcend them. While some discussants denied that the recently formed unofficial "voluntary associations" were legitimate "bearers of pluralism" (and dismissed their leaders as "aggressive mediocrities"), others welcomed them as harbingers of expanding democracy. While the more cautious kept reiterating the need for a pluralism "of opinions," others insisted on a pluralism "of action, of structure, of organization." While some expressed support for encouraging the growth of "socialist pluralism," others wondered why the adjective was necessary (Roundtable, 1988c, 1989c). Given the ongoing confrontation between these conflicting positions, the insistence of the more conservative discussants that "healthy pluralism" within the party defined the appropriate limits of political pluralism seems to have acted as an invitation to supporters of a multiparty system to make their case explicitly and with no holds barred. What were some of the principal arguments invoked to make that case?

For B. Kurashvili (1989a, 1989b), whose reformist credentials were originally earned in the pre-Gorbachev years, the one-party system—as a relic of Stalinism—had become a principal source of the general crisis of Soviet socialism. The monopoly of political power associated with one-party rule ("like every monopoly, and even more than other types of monopoly") generated "decay" in the system. The fact that the party had not had an adequate "political line" for decades was rooted in the one-party system, since the latter permitted the party to adopt and implement its policies "without criticism from the outside." The monopolistic nature of the political system meant that there could be no "independent monitoring" of party rule (a factor making for widespread corruption among the political leadership) and that substantial sections of the population were deprived of political representation. Kurashvili insisted that it was time to recognize that "the interests of society are higher than the interests of the party" (1989a, p. 23). More specifically, this meant that it would be desirable for the Soviet people to have two or more competing (and occasionally collaborating) "political vanguards" from which to choose, so that power could be entrusted to the one proposing "the more rational path of development." Kurashvili was not disturbed by the prospect that nonsocialist parties might enter the resulting political competition, nor did he regard extensive "privatization" as a necessary condition for the functioning of a multiparty system in a socialist democracy.[6]

Explicit support for a multiparty system in Soviet discussions of pluralism was commonly accompanied by the abandonment of other key elements of traditional Soviet ideology. The unquestioning acceptance of one-party rule had long been a pillar of that ideology, and it is difficult to imagine that its rejection would not have had a "ripple effect" on other critical components of the larger set of accepted beliefs. The remarks of V.P. Kiselev, a participant in a Moscow State University roundtable discussion of pluralism early in 1989, provide an illustration of this unraveling process. Kiselev found it "shameful" that some discussants had opposed political pluralism in "the broad sense," i.e., in the sense of recognizing the legitimacy of a political opposition operating in the context of a multiparty system. While such arrangements could not be implemented immediately in the Soviet Union, this was clearly the direction in which Soviet society had to move. Was it really the case, asked Kiselev, that countries like Chile, South Korea, Algeria, and Burma were ready for a multiparty system, but "we are not" (Roundtable, 1989c, p. 52)? He appealed to the party to set the stage for the emergence of a multiparty system by itself becoming a "model of democracy," a process that would be promoted by recognizing the right of distinct groups in the party to organize their own factions and issue their own platforms. It should come as no surprise, therefore, that Kiselev also made it clear that he accepted the principle of "ideological pluralism," that he regarded the vision of a communist future in which the division of labor would be overcome as "utopian," and that the time had come to recognize the "historical limitations" not only of the earlier Soviet model of socialism but of "socialism itself as a moral, political, and economic ideal" (ibid., pp. 48, 50–51). The theme of pluralism clearly lent itself to some remarkable breaks with traditional Soviet thinking. It also seems worth noting that Kiselev's remarks were made from "within," i.e., in the course of a discussion organized by the party committee of Moscow State University.

Of special interest was the manner in which a new economic orthodoxy—the model of an efficiently functioning market mechanism—was also invoked to make the case for political pluralism and a multiparty system. The writings of V. Amelin (1989, 1990) provide the best illustration of this approach. Amelin introduced the concept of a "political market" into Soviet discussions of political institutions. "Just as the dismantling of the command-administrative system in the economy is linked with the appearance of different forms of property and a market mechanism of exchange between independent commodity producers, so in political life there have appeared independent political subjects expressing the interests of different social forces" (Amelin, 1990, p. 102). Referring to the situation prevailing at the end of the 1980s, the "independent political subjects" Amelin had in mind included the various people's fronts and informal associations that had already emerged, as well as new political parties that he expected would shortly appear on the "political market." The extension of such a market was to be welcomed, for it promoted the open nature (*publichnost'*) of political life, enriched the range of political concepts and ideas circulating in society, and helped prevent the high degree of concentration of political power that had prevailed in the past. For Amelin, there was no basic conflict between the principles of socialism on the one hand and "commodity-money relations" (essentially a market mechanism) and a multiparty system on the other (1989, p. 203). Indeed, he seemed to suggest that the assimilation of market mechanisms (in both the political and economic spheres) would be a source of strength for Soviet society. "Just as a national economic market ensures stability in the functioning of the national economy, so a national political market ensures stability in the political system" (1990, p. 105). Amelin's unbounded confidence in the beneficent consequences of a "political market" was obviously reinforced by his finding that significant portions of public opinion (including almost a quarter of sampled party activists) reacted favorably to the prospects of a multiparty system (ibid.).

4. We noted earlier that some advocates of political pluralism and an emancipated civil society (A.M. Migranian, in particular) sought to make their case without invoking the need for a multiparty system. But it must also be recognized that some participants in these discussions who explicitly accepted the need for a multiparty system were hardly guided by democratic sentiments. For the economist A. Sergeev (1989) such a system was more in the nature of a regrettable necessity than an indicator of the growing maturity of Soviet society. A multiparty system was now justified insofar as recent years had seen the emergence of social groups with "incompatible economic interests." Sergeev contrasted the position of the mass of the Soviet population (who lived "from wage payment to wage payment") with an emergent "plutocracy, a new Soviet bourgeoisie" (*sovbury*) actively engaged in the private accumulation of capital. A principal source of the latter groups was the activity of cooperatives (their operations "exploited" both consumers and their hired hands). Some elements of the new plutocracy were essentially dealers in the "shadow economy," whose operations had been extended in recent years as a result of the expanding role of cooperatives. In this situation Sergeev recognized that "objective conditions" were appropriate for the existence of two parties: a communist party (reflecting the interests of workers, collective farmers, and the technical-engineering intelligentsia employed largely at state factories), and an "antisocialist party" rooted in the new exploiting strata and the "intellectual bourgeoisie" (intellectuals who supported a transition to capitalism). Thus, while accepting the legitimacy of a departure from the one-party system (and it should be noted that he did so well before the party itself adopted such a position), Sergeev was clearly a critic of the economic policies that made such a departure necessary. This was surely a case where the readiness to accept a multiparty system did not reflect the flowering of a democratic consciousness. But it does seem appropriate to distinguish this reaction from what we earlier characterized as the "minimalist response" to the issue of pluralism.

Our review of these discussions has revealed a considerable diversity of Soviet responses to the issue of political pluralism. But whatever their differences on the substance of this issue, the great majority of discussants—perhaps all—would almost certainly have agreed with the sociologist Bestuzhev-Lada (Roundtable, 1988c, p. 8) that the common point of departure in thinking about pluralism must be "the presumption of nonpunishability for thinking differently." While the acceptance of this principle may not strike all observers as a great achievement, the discussion reviewed above would probably have been impossible without it.

Introduction to a Future Controversy

All of the discussions related to the theme of political democratization reviewed thus far required that the participants come to terms with some old orthodoxies. It was virtually impossible to confront seriously concepts like civil society, bourgeois democracy, and political pluralism without (explicitly or implicitly) being forced to reassess traditional Soviet views on the nature of the state and the party in Soviet society and the possibilities for working-class political representation in capitalist-dominated societies. But none of the Soviet literature examined up to this point explicitly questioned whether political democracy was possible in a predominantly socialist economy. Among the first to challenge the compatibility of political democracy and socialism directly was the economist L. Piiasheva (1989). In effect, Piiasheva's comments on this theme were part of a broader critique of social-democratic and welfare-state economic policies in Western Europe. Unlike most of the earlier Soviet literature on the social-democratic tradition, however, Piiasheva's appraisal of this variety of socialism was essentially a critique from the "right." Thus, while focusing mainly on the alleged failures of traditional welfare-state redistributive economic policies—policies that mistakenly diverted excessive resources from the "strong and competitive" to the "weak and noncompetitive"— Piiasheva also sought to alert Soviet readers to the potentially

dangerous political consequences of the social-democratic movement. "We need to take very seriously the warning served by
Hayek . . . to the effect that even a peaceful, social-democratic
road to socialism leads to total collectivism, socialization, statization, a planned command economy, monopoly, and the suppression of individualism, democracy, and individual freedom"
(ibid., p. 99). Piiasheva's point, quite simply, was that the increasingly popular conception of "democratic socialism" was
self-contradictory.

Thus, whatever its limitations, the democratization of Soviet
political discourse in the late 1980s was not confined to those
who argued within the Marxist or even socialist traditions.
Piiasheva's critical comments on the social-democratic movement reflected the early stages of a controversy between contending intellectual and political currents (social democrats and
"liberal democrats" in the West European sense) whose emergence to prominence in the Soviet Union would have seemed
well-nigh inconceivable a few years earlier. We return to some of
the principal manifestations of these intellectual currents in chapter
5, where we examine the desanctification of Marxism-Leninism.

Notes

1. While our review of this discussion has drawn on what might be called
the "scholarly" literature (which obviously has a comparatively limited circula-
tion), similar views have appeared in popular newspapers. One illustration is
Liubimov (1989).

2. It also seems of some interest that the poll that revealed sizable support
for a multiparty system was conducted by a teacher at the Moscow Higher
Party School. He seemed to favor the emergence of such a system, which he
regarded as being no more in conflict with the principles of socialism than
reliance on a market mechanism (Amelin, 1989, p. 203).

3. For one example of a relatively positive reaction to Migranian's views,
see Vilchek (1989).

4. Some critics of this view wondered why it could not also have been
invoked by defenders of czarism earlier in the century.

5. In Migranian's view all classes and social groups in Soviet society
shared the "basic values of Marxism and socialism." Hence there was no need
to return to multiparty arrangements "in the old sense," i.e., in the sense of

ideologically polarized, "class parties." Thus his apparent readiness to rely on the equivalent of "interest groups" as instruments of political pluralism. See Migranian, 1988b, p. 120.

6. He did, however, favor the transfer of public property to "group possession" (*grupovoe vladenie*) on a long-term basis or in perpetuity. It is worth noting that Kurashvili was able to make his case for a multiparty system most fully in an Estonian party journal (1989a), although his general sympathy for such a system was also unambiguously expressed in an article published in the principal journal of the Academy of Sciences Institute of State and Law (1989b).

4

The Issue of "Social Justice"

As in the immediate pre-Gorbachev period (see chapter 1), Soviet discussions of "social justice" in the late 1980s focused largely on the issue of inequalities in economic status—essentially the issue of distributive justice. These discussions were enriched by the release of more than the normal volume of data on the magnitude of certain types of economic inequalities (especially on the distribution of savings accounts) and by enhanced opportunities for the discussants to confront the sensitive issue of "privileges" for favored social groups. Although a systematic review of available data on income and wealth inequalities is not part of our objective here, such material will be invoked below when it serves to clarify the positions adopted by the principal antagonists in Soviet controversies on distributive justice. Recent years have witnessed a direct confrontation between advocates of reduced inequalities in economic status and those who see the excessive "leveling" of Soviet incomes as a principal source of the country's economic problems. We shall consider the arguments of both groups.

Of special interest are conflicting Soviet views on the relationship between democratization and inequalities in income and wealth. From a Western perspective it seems natural to associate the extension of democracy with increased equalities in the distribution of goods and services. Some Soviet observers are obviously inclined to accept this view. But for other participants in these discussions—especially "free-market" enthusiasts—the critical question is whether democratization will facilitate or impede the acceptance of the increased income inequalities urgently required for economic recovery. Clearly, recent Soviet discussions of issues related to distributive justice merit close examination.

For and Against "Active Redistribution"

The explicit repudiation of egalitarianism or wage leveling (*uravnilovka*) has long been an almost obligatory element in Soviet discussions of wage and income structures. But this has not stopped some commentators from focusing their criticism on what they obviously regard as unjustifiably large inequalities in economic status. Indeed, as noted in chapter 1, the accession of Gorbachev was followed by an "escalation" in attacks on allegedly excessive inequalities in the distribution of income and wealth. Perhaps the clearest illustration of such attacks in the name of distributive justice may be found in the writings of the sociologist V.Z. Rogovin. These are worth examining not only because they express—at least implicitly—the egalitarian sentiments often said to be typical of many Soviet citizens but also because Rogovin's work became a principal target of advocates of increased income differentiation.

Distributive justice under Soviet conditions, argued Rogovin in 1985–86, required the establishment not only of a socially guaranteed minimum, but also of a "socially permissible maximum" family income per capita. The need to set such a maximum derived from the general principle that a socialist society must impose certain limits on income differentiation. Distributive justice was simply incompatible with a situation in which particular individuals had "unlimited opportunities for accumulation and consumption" (Rogovin, 1985a, p. 51). Rogovin did not specify the precise level at which the legal maximum should be set, but he suggested several mechanisms that would presumably help to implement the concept. One would require all citizens of working age to submit declarations of all their sources of income to financial authorities, with "serious" (but unspecified) consequences in store for those who sought to conceal portions of their income. This requirement would be supplemented by a new scale of progressive income taxation specifically designed to apply not only to wage income received from employment at state enterprises but also to income that Rogovin claimed was "very weakly covered by taxation": income from sales of output of personal household plots, from the rental of housing space, from the provision of personal services, etc. But the critical feature of Rogovin's proposed tax measure was the incorporation of top rates that would provide for the "effective taxation of excessive incomes" and would embody the principle of a maximum permissible (posttax) income.

Along with this principle, distributive justice for Rogovin also required a closer correspondence between inequalities in economic rewards and people's relative "labor contribution." This was not simply the usual appeal to combat various forms of illegal income—those commonly summed up in references to "bribery, speculation, and embezzlement." A closer fit between relative incomes and relative work contribution also required the curtailment and redistribution of certain categories of legal nonlabor income. Here Rogovin singled out "the unlimited right of inheritance" of monetary savings and personal property as illustrating sources of real income that permitted some people to lead "a prosperous mode of life" for extended periods without contributing their own labor to society's production requirements. Hence it would be appropriate, according to Rogovin, to impose a "sizable" inheritance tax whenever the value of the transferred savings or property substantially exceeded the "vital resources" available to the bulk of the Soviet population (ibid.).

As these discussions unfolded, it became clear that Rogovin's policy proposal was not primarily directed against the principle of inheritance as such but was essentially a response to the unequal "starting positions" of young people associated with the highly unequal distribution of personal savings among the Soviet population. Rogovin cited the results of a study of the distribution of savings in the Latvian republic that would be invoked repeatedly in the late 1980s as symbolic of excessive inequalities in economic status (1985b, 1986; Lachinov, 1988). The study's findings apparently showed that approximately one-half the value of savings deposits in the republic was concentrated in 3 percent of the accounts, with the average value of the accounts in this 3 percent group exceeding 20,000 rubles. It seemed obvious to Rogovin that such sums often reflected access to nonlabor sources of income—legal or illegal. However, the critical issue for this representative of Soviet egalitarianism was not the sources of such savings but their highly unequal distribution. Even if the high levels of savings of this upper 3 percent were derived strictly from labor incomes, "such considerable differentiation, it seems to me, should not exist in a socialist society" (Rogovin, 1985b).

Whatever the prospects for economic growth in the near future, it could not be expected to generate the resources required to establish relatively equal "starting conditions" for youngsters drawn from families with highly unequal incomes and savings. Hence the need to rely on an "active redistributive policy" (presumably the kind embodied in Rogovin's proposals for setting upper limits on incomes and on the right to inherent property and financial assets). Assistance to low-income groups would have to come at least in part from financial resources diverted from the more well-to-do.

The egalitarian sentiments of this sociologist were also reflected in his readiness to pronounce judgment on what constituted "normal" income differentials and the modest consumption patterns appropriate to the current state of Soviet society. Thus the prevailing ratio of approximately 3 : 1 for the decile coefficient of wage differentiation in state enterprises[1] (a commonly used Soviet indicator of the relationship between comparatively "high" and "low" wages) was characterized by Rogovin as "completely normal" (1986, p. 12). The problem, in his view, was that the actual differentiation of overall incomes (including nonlabor incomes) and consumption opportunities (after allowance for transmission of savings and property through inheritance) was obviously in excess of this 3 : 1 ratio. But the sense of distributive justice conveyed in Rogovin's writings did not require exclusive reliance on sophisticated statistical measures of inequality. Intuitive assessments of a just distribution of particular goods could also be relied upon. For example, it seemed obvious that the possession of a private automobile by a miner or a professor could hardly be considered as excessive. "But the same automobile given by a father as a gift to his twenty-year-old son who has not earned one kopeck in his life suggests that social justice has been violated" (ibid., p. 15). In the same spirit, in his comments on readers' letters, Rogovin repeatedly conveyed his sympathy with those readers who affirmed their own adherence to a "modest lifestyle" and expressed their resentment at neighbors who flaunted their wealth (especially when the latter was derived from "underground production"). Rogovin's egalitarian sentiments were clearly inseparable from his criticism of expenditure patterns that appeared to embody "consumerism" in the Soviet context.

The explicit rejection of Rogovin's brand of egalitarianism and a completely different perspective on issues of economic inequality may be found in the writings of G. Lisichkin (1986, 1987, 1988). Particularly objectionable, for this economist, was Rogovin's appeal for an "active redistributive policy." Advocates of redistribution, in Lisichkin's view, failed to distinguish between two distinct problems in the sphere of economic inequality. Obviously it was necessary to combat the embezzlement and "plunder" of public property and to extract the illegal and often substantial incomes derived from such activities. But no less important was the need to encourage and increase monetary rewards for "high-quality" work, to provide adequate supplies of consumers' goods (moreover, the kind that corresponded to "the tastes of buyers"), and to strengthen the "protection of personal property" (Lisichkin, 1986). Clearly, Lisichkin's concern was that the demand for "active redistribution" might lend itself to a policy that would penalize precisely those groups of conscientious and competent workers whose incomes should be increased (or at the very least, not decreased) if work motivation was to be strengthened. Furthermore, he asked, what particular groups of the poor or deprived (*maloobespechennye*) were to be aided by the proposed redistributive policies? Society should certainly seek to increase its assistance to the "sick, the elderly, and the disabled." But in those cases where a social group's low income reflected its "unwillingness to raise its work skills," a simple redistribution of income at the expense of more well-to-do (and hence, presumably, more diligent) work groups was the wrong way to proceed. For Lisichkin it seemed obvious that low-wage groups should be placed in a situation where a rise in their incomes would have to be preceded by an increase in their labor productivity (1988, p. 213). The essential danger embodied in Rogovin's approach was that it linked an improvement in the economic status of low-income groups to redistributive policies rather than to the improved work performance of these groups.

Indeed, for Lisichkin, redistributive policies had already proceeded too far and were damaging the economy. The main problem was not unjustified inequalities in relative incomes but rather the opposite—inadequate income differentials for groups of workers making highly unequal contributions to economic output. The particular manner in which Lisichkin defended and elaborated this point reflected a view of the Soviet work force that permeated the antiegalitarian literature of the late 1980s. Lisichkin invoked the case of two neighboring farms—a collective farm and a state farm—that exhibited markedly different levels of economic performance. The collective farm was highly profitable, while the state farm operated at a loss with crop yields only some one-fifth to one-third the level achieved at the more efficient collective farm (and with livestock productivity similarly much higher at the latter farm). But the critical point repeatedly stressed in Lisichkin's account was that the monthly earnings of state-farm workers were only slightly below (by ten rubles) the earnings level prevailing at the much more efficient and profitable collective farm, and living conditions were essentially the same for the two groups. What accounted for the inferior economic performance of the state farm? Lisichkin's explanation focused almost exclusively on one factor—the indifference, irresponsibility, and incompetence of the state farm's work force, aided and abetted by a similarly incompetent managerial staff. The bulk of this work force was characterized by Lisichkin as consisting of "loafers" (*lodyry*) and a slightly less irresponsible group whose principal concern was "to put in the necessary time" (*otrabotat' lish ot "sikh" do "sikh"*). As for the few who were prepared to work conscientiously and competently—the state farm's workers were not a homogeneous group, acknowledged Lisichkin—they were forced to adapt themselves to the "drab mediocrity" of the majority who wanted "nothing more than peace and quiet" (Lisichkin, 1987; 1988, pp. 227–28). Although Lisichkin did not bother to spell out the characteristics of the work force at the highly profitable collective farm in any detail, the obvious implication was that the latter's high yield reflected a much higher quality of work effort and skill.

Thus a very different conception of basic group divisions emerged in the writings of Rogovin and Lisichkin. For the former, the principal division was that between the more fortunate or privileged (whether because of nonlabor incomes, access to "closed" channels of distribution, or unusually high labor earnings) and the disadvantaged. Lisichkin, on the other hand, saw a work force sharply divided between those who "knew how to work" and those who did not (and were not particularly interested in learning), with comparatively small earnings differentials between these two groups. The proximity in earnings levels of the two groups (as symbolized by the case of the two farms) meant that a "sizable chunk" was already being extracted from the efficient and conscientious in order to "feed the slackers" (*neradivye*). Thus for Lisichkin, calls for a policy of additional "active redistribution" threatened to aggravate an already unhealthy situation. Was it not obvious that "dependents" never learn to work productively and "soon lose the habit of standing

on their own feet . . . ?" Lisichkin's intense antiegalitarianism
was not so much an appeal to dispense with the general principle
of redistribution of income as a call for a sharp reversal in the
direction of that redistribution, a change in favor of those "who
want to and know how to work competently" (1987). In the
context of his comparison of the two farms, it meant that the
differential in their average earnings should be on the order of
3–5 : 1 rather than the insignificant ten rubles per month (which
obviously reflected subsidies to the "weak" state farm). Such
earnings differentials would not only be in greater accord with
social justice, since they would then approximate differences in
labor productivity, they would also act as a spur to the work
effort of both higher and lower income groups.

But the issue for this opponent of wage leveling was more than
simply the need for increased inequalities in money incomes. In a
formulation that begged for elaboration (which it did not receive,
at least in the article in which it was invoked), Lisichkin declared
that the time had come for the competent and the skilled to be
given the right "to order the music" for which they paid (ibid.).
Without speculating on the variety of messages this formulation
was intended to convey, it seems clear that at the very least it did
not reflect the concern with "consumerism" that was apparent in
Rogovin's writings.

Whatever the strength of Lisichkin's case for selected increases in earnings inequalities, some of his responses to
Rogovin's arguments seemed to deny the possibility that excessive inequalities in economic status could be a legitimate concern
in the late 1980s. It was almost as though the consequences of a
stultifying egalitarianism were so all-embracing and the evidence
of a sharp dichotomy between conscientious workers and the
"slackers" was so obvious that they constituted a ready rebuttal
to any appeals for limiting or reducing inequalities in income and
wealth. Lisichkin's response to Rogovin's invocation of the
highly unequal holdings of savings accounts in the Latvian republic provides a case in point. For Rogovin, it will be recalled,
such inequalities appeared to justify a "sizable" inheritance tax

on transfers of relatively large accounts. For Lisichkin, however, another consideration was dominant. "What if this 3 percent of depositors [those holding about one-half the value of all accounts] are people of crystal-clear honesty? What if this is that small part of the republic's population that, long before the adoption of decisive measures against drunkenness and alcoholism, voluntarily led a sober mode of life while the rest simply were drinking up what they earned?" (Lisichkin, 1986; 1987, p. 219). Lisichkin's thinking on these matters was apparently so dominated by his distinction between competent workers and "slackers" (in this case, "drunkards") and so absorbed with the larger battle against the negative impact of egalitarian sentiments that it is difficult to take seriously his response to Rogovin on the issue of the distribution of savings.

Nor was the Latvian data invoked by Rogovin the only evidence of substantial inequalities in holdings of financial assets, inequalities that could not readily be explained by differences in Soviet citizens' "labor contribution" or their predilection for alcohol. Thus A.N. Shokhin, drawing on sample data for several regions, estimated that "1 percent of the population had accumulated in its hands from one-quarter to one-third of monetary savings" (1989, p. 217). Another estimate provided by an official of the Soviet savings-bank system suggested that at the beginning of 1989 less than one-fifth of the system's accounts held more than three-fifths of the total value of savings deposits (Valiuzhenich, 1990). Since large depositors tended to hold several separate accounts, the concentration of the country's savings among bank depositors was greater than indicated by these figures. Whatever else may explain this highly unequal distribution of savings, two factors essentially ignored by Lisichkin surely played some role: "criminal" or illegal sources of income (this factor was especially stressed by Shokhin, who regarded it as playing a significant role in the differentiation of incomes and hence of savings), and the variety of mechanisms subsumed under the label of "privileges" (to be discussed below). In any case, Lisichkin's somewhat one-dimensional view of the principal source of savings inequalities does not appear to have been shared by other participants in these discussions.

But there was also an aspect of Rogovin's position that conflicted with the views expressed in most of the serious Soviet literature on economic inequalities. Rogovin, it will be recalled, regarded the prevailing ratio of approximately 3 : 1 for the decile coefficient of wage differentiation in state enterprises as "completely normal" (figures released subsequently showed that it actually stood at 3.3 : 1 in 1986—Rimashevskaia, 1989, p. 370). The implication was that prevailing skill and occupational differentials in labor earnings were roughly adequate and that there was no strong case for widening such differentials as a means of improving work incentives. On this score Rogovin appeared to stand alone (just as Lisichkin seemed alone in his interpretation of the savings data discussed above). All the more serious Soviet scholars in this area appeared to favor an increase in skill differentials in labor incomes in the late 1980s (Mikul'skii, 1988; Shokhin, 1989; Rimashevskaia, 1989). But it does not follow from this that they all favored increased inequality in the overall distribution of Soviet real incomes. The point is that such inequality was at least as much (if not more) affected by "criminal" incomes and officially authorized "privileges" as by state-established money wage rates (Mikul'skii, 1988, p. 12; Shokhin, 1989, p. 224). Hence an increase in skill differentials in labor earnings, as called for by most participants in these discussions, would have been perfectly compatible with a decline in overall income inequality[2]—assuming vigorous measures directed against illegal incomes and legal "privileges." Indeed, in the final years of the 1980s, the theme of social justice (more precisely, social *injustice*) was invoked most frequently in connection with those inequalities in real income commonly associated with "privileges" and related practices that made the poor pay more for essential goods than the well-to-do. These are the issues to which we now turn.

Toward the Implementation of Equal Access

There was a symmetrical quality to the critical Soviet literature on inequalities in economic rewards in the late 1980s. Whether the principal target of criticism was wage leveling (*uravnilovka*) or allegedly excessive inequalities, there was an underlying consistency in the criteria explicitly or implicitly invoked to justify these assessments. Thus if we examine the logic (as distinct from the rhetoric) of the attacks on the evil of egalitarianism, they rested on essentially two grounds. One was the simple notion that wage differentials that substantially understated differences in the "quantity and quality" of work performed represented a departure from social justice. Thus the latter concept was basically identified with "the labor principle of distribution" (Rimashevskaia, 1989, p. 366). This does not mean that all the Soviet literature on this theme simplistically assumed that differences in people's contribution (through labor expended) to output were always precisely quantifiable or that social justice in the sphere of income distribution meant no more than gearing wage differentials to differences in work performance. At least the more sophisticated literature in this area sought to elaborate a concept of distributive justice that simultaneously embraced both "the labor principle of distribution" and the principle of providing all citizens with equal opportunity for self-development—in Rimashevskaia's words, "equal opportunity for each to realize his abilities on the basis of the constitutionally guaranteed right to an education, to work, to health care, to housing" (ibid., p. 365). But more typically the core meaning of the common attack on wage leveling as a departure from social justice was that it violated the principle that "he who works better should also live better" (Barabasheva and Vengerov, 1988, p. 192). The second principal ground for targeting allegedly narrow wage differentials, obviously related to the first, was their presumed negative impact on work incentives and work performance. Nowhere was this argument pressed more persistently than in the writings of Lisichkin reviewed above. The practice of subsidizing the unskilled and the incompetent at the expense of those "who know how to work"—as reflected in the relatively narrow differentials in their earnings—served as a work disincentive for both groups and was a principal factor explaining the widespread evidence of indifferent work performance.

But as the decade drew to a close, the same two concepts—social (in)justice and work (dis)incentives—were increasingly invoked in the literature directed against what appeared to be the very opposite of wage leveling, namely, unjustified inequalities in the consumption opportunities of various groups of citizens. We are not referring here primarily to the differentials in money income and savings inequalities singled out by Rogovin but to certain distributional mechanisms characterized by the unequal access of different social groups to various types of retail markets and other channels of acquisition of consumer goods and services. Here the target of critics was the unequal purchasing power of the ruble, where the value of the latter was significantly dependent upon the recipients' area of residence, economic sector of employment, and official position in the state-party hierarchy.

There was no mystery about the nature of the particular distributional mechanisms that ensured preferential treatment for selected social groups (Kirichenko and Shmarov, 1988; Shokhin et al., 1988; Shokhin, 1989). One illustration is provided by the highly skewed location of state food shops (with their relatively low, subsidized prices) on the one hand and the principal "commercial" outlets (higher-priced cooperatives and kolkhoz markets) on the other. Residents of Moscow, Leningrad, and other large cities (the capitals of the union republics, for example) were much more adequately supplied by the low-priced outlets than residents of relatively small urban centers. Not only were state food shops scarcer in the smaller cities, but they were more likely to be short of meat and dairy products than state stores in large urban centers, thus increasing the dependence of people in less-urbanized areas on the higher-priced "commercial" outlets. The significance of this is enhanced when it is realized that wages "as a rule" were lower in small towns than in large urban centers (Kirichenko and Shmarov, 1988). A similar impact on the distribution of real income stemmed from the practice of giving enterprises in high-priority sectors the right to place orders for food supplies to be distributed to employees at the work site at state-subsidized prices. Those who benefited from this practice were concentrated mainly in comparatively high-wage sectors like heavy industry, defense, and electronics and also included the staffs of government ministries and other "solid" organizations (ibid.; Shokhin, 1989, p. 197). Thus, once again, higher-paid groups' preferential access to low-cost outlets for scarce goods reinforced the dependence of lower-income groups on the higher-priced "commercial" markets. For example, Shokhin (1989, p. 223) found that the more well-to-do purchased more than three-quarters of their meat supplies at subsidized state prices, while the comparable figure for lower-income groups was "barely more than one-half." Little wonder that the principal sources on which we rely seem to agree that on a per capita basis high-income groups benefited substantially more from state subsidies than low-income groups.[3]

But the most blatant, and certainly the most provocative, cases of unequal access were embodied in the consumption privileges available to groups of sufficiently high "rank" in the occupational structure. These "official-status" markets, as Shokhin called them (ibid., p. 218), embraced not only "closed" distribution channels in the form of special shops reserved for the *nomenklatura* and others in "executive" positions (and typically carrying a higher quality and wider range of consumer goods than were available in other marketing channels) but also included privileged vacation facilities and medical services (ibid., 1989, pp. 195, 197, 218, 222; Rimashevskaia, 1989, p. 373; Barabasheva and Vengerov, 1988, p. 214).

Clearly, it was not difficult for the critics of such practices in the late 1980s to demonstrate that they conflicted with the traditional, more or less official Soviet canons of social justice. Whether the basis for the particular group's preferential access to scarce, comparatively low-cost goods and services was size of city, economic sector, or (especially) "rank" in officialdom, this was hardly the equivalent of distribution in accordance with labor contribution. For some critics the "basic injustice" associated with the unequal purchasing power of the ruble—the unequal opportunity of groups to convert their rubles into real goods and services—was that it created the opportunity for bureaucratic strata to appropriate for themselves the labor of other social groups (Barabasheva and Vengerov, 1988, p. 225).

But of special interest was the manner in which the widespread perception of unjust "bureaucratic privileges" was also invoked to account for the negative work attitudes and indifferent work performance commonly observed at Soviet enterprises. For the economist S. Dzarasov (1990, p. 44), for example, the "special supplies and special services" available to high-ranking executives and officials were a principal source of the "total disinterest" of Soviet workers in efficient, high-quality job performance. Some of the critical literature on unequal access and its negative consequences for work incentives appears to have been implicitly directed against Lisichkin's characterization of Soviet workers (see above) and his almost exclusive focus on the evil of inadequate wage differentials between "good" and "bad" workers: "It is no accident that many workers reduce their work efforts, but this is not because they are bad workers, or lazy, or want to receive unearned wages, etc., as some scholars and journalists think. The problem is more worrisome. Many workers simply do not want to work for bureaucratic structures, since the injustice in the realization of wages ... is so obvious" (Barabasheva and Vengerov, 1988, p. 225).

The context of these remarks makes it clear that the "injustice" the authors had in mind was associated with the various forms of privileged access to consumption opportunities discussed above. It would be a vast oversimplification, of course, to equate these attacks on privilege with an appeal for an egalitarian type of income distribution. But at the very least the emphasis here was markedly different than that found in the writings of Lisichkin and other apostles of antiegalitarianism (for example, Radaev, 1988; Cherniak, 1988), for whom wage-leveling policies were almost invariably the only, or the principal, obstacles to improved work incentives. The alternative view was clearly reflected in the writings of Shokhin, whose work served as a major source of documentation on the regressive impact on income distribution of the various mechanisms of unequal access. For Shokhin, two types of policies were required to "normalize" inequalities in real income: one would raise the general level of labor incomes, and the other would eliminate the "multiplicity of consumer markets," thereby creating "uniform conditions for the realization of earned incomes for all population groups" (1989, p. 233). Thus, whatever the urgency of increased differentiation of labor incomes—and Shokhin clearly accepted the need for such increased differentiation—it was no less important to eliminate a host of prevailing inequalities in real income opportunities unrelated to labor contribution, i.e., inequalities linked to the unequal purchasing power of the ruble for various social groups.

An additional aspect of the literature directed against bureaucratic privilege is worth noting at this point. Writing in 1988, Barabasheva and Vengerov argued that the democratization of Soviet public life, repeatedly proclaimed at the time as a major element of *perestroika*, must also encompass the "democratization of distributive relations" (pp. 199–204). Despite the novelty of the latter concept, its essential meaning was fairly clear. Such democratization implied eliminating, or at least reducing, the domination of bureaucratic strata over decisions bearing on income distribution, including their right to ensure their own consumption privileges. Decision-making authority on distributional issues would now be increasingly shifted from "higher to lower echelons," i.e., to economic enterprises and their work collectives, comparable to the shifts taking place in decisions bearing on selection of managers, pricing, and the management of production. Thus the "democratization of distribution" appeared to promise reduced inequalities in the distribution of power and—to the extent that it implied the reduction of the unjust consumption privileges of the "higher echelons"—reduced inequalities in the distribution of real income as well. But other participants in these discussions focused on a rather different and more uncertain connection between democratization and economic inequality.

Democracy, Property, and Inequality

Whatever the possible equalizing impact of eliminating or reducing privileged access to "closed" channels of supply, there was another theme that dominated Soviet discussions of income differentiation on the threshold of the nineties. The principal types of economic reforms then being projected and introduced, namely, the transition to a market-directed system and the diversification and privatization of property ownership, were commonly regarded as necessarily linked to increased inequalities in economic rewards. But would the concurrent democratization of Soviet political and intellectual life make such inequalities more acceptable to the Soviet public? Or would "populist" excesses, nourished by traditional egalitarian sentiments and now given an opportunity for open political expression, undo the positive impact on economic performance that could be expected from increased income differentiation? These were the issues posed and directly confronted in the writings of the economist G. Popov. Of special interest is the manner in which his views, particularly his defense of increased economic inequalities, represented both a continuity and a break with traditional Soviet views on distributional issues (Popov, 1989, 1990a, 1990b).

In the reformed economy now so urgently needed (for Popov this was essentially a market-directed system with substantial "denationalization" of productive property), incomes would be determined by "the results of labor." There could hardly be a more familiar formulation in the Soviet context. But Popov was quick to point out its changed meaning in the new situation. The "results" in question would be assessed by the market and not according to the usual criterion—the degree of fulfillment of a plan assignment. This meant that incomes of enterprises (and thus presumably of their workers) could be substantially affected by factors like the novelty of the product and "distortions in the structure of the economy" (here Popov apparently had in mind product shortages and/or monopolistic powers of firms in particular sectors). Moreover, the normal functioning of a market system meant that relatively high income groups would soon include those engaged in "intermediary" or middleman-type activities (*posrednichestvo*), in buying and selling, "the investment of money," in organizational and entrepreneurial activities. What concerned Popov was obvious. Some of these were precisely the kinds of activities long identified by broad sections of the Soviet public with "nonlabor incomes." But especially urgent, in Popov's view, was the need for the reformed economy to create increased opportunities for income "from previous labor," for "money yielding additional money"—essentially euphemisms for various forms of property income. Popov was fully aware that this was a highly sensitive issue and that the readiness of the Soviet public to accept such a policy was in question. Hence his appeal to readers to recognize the enormous real costs of continued restrictions on personal-property income and ownership: "We must reflect: Are not the chronic misfortunes of administrative socialism—indifference to property (previous labor), the waste of natural resources, the ecological crisis, the irresponsible attitude toward materials and equipment—connected to the notion that only current labor performs a creative role in the formation of value?" (Popov, 1989).

Essentially similar sentiments, perhaps formulated in somewhat cruder and more direct terms, began to appear in the most "official" of publications. The message conveyed in an article in *Kommunist* as the decade of the eighties drew to a close provides a case in point. The message was that the traditionally contemptuous Soviet attitude toward the "huckster" (*torgash*), the "intermediary," the financier, was an anachronism. Unless Soviet citizens began to "treat people who know how to 'make money' with respect," they could not expect to live in "an effective economy" (Volkonskii, 1990, pp. 62–63). Clearly, this was an appeal to abandon the deeply ingrained suspicion of high earnings that was at the very core of popular egalitarianism.

But it was Popov who formulated what was obviously a critical issue in the most challenging terms: Would the unprecedented political democratization that Soviet society so urgently required block or facilitate public acceptance of the substantial increase in economic inequality that seemed inherent in the projected economic reforms? On the one hand, only a democratic version of *perestroika* could be taken seriously. "There can be no compromises in the sphere of democracy" (Popov, 1989). Thus victory over the "apparatus of bureaucratic socialism" and the implementation of a market-directed, substantially privatized economy required the active support and involvement of the masses, presumably acting through newly established democratic institutions in which they had a political voice. Moreover, it would be wrong to conceal from the masses that the new economy would be characterized by considerable income differentiation, with "one part of society being able to earn ten times more than another." Popov's hope was that the Soviet public's level of "culture" was sufficient for it to understand that the increased wealth of some would provide the foundation for "an increase in the general level of well-being of all." The positive association between increased economic inequality and higher average living standards was apparently so obvious to Popov that it hardly seemed necessary to demonstrate or elaborate the point. Similarly, the increased personal freedom and improvement in the quality of life associated with democratization should operate to make the necessary increase in economic inequality more acceptable to the public.

However, Popov also stressed that the potential benefits of reformist economic policies, including the benefits of increased economic inequality, were by no means assured. Paradoxically, this was related to the rapid increase in opportunities for political self-expression. The principal danger was a familiar one—the ever-present and destructive impact of Soviet egalitarian sentiments. There were still "a considerable number of people who would more readily agree to live poorly, rather than to live better if this meant that someone else would be even better off than they" (ibid.). (One cannot help but wonder whether any of the numerous public opinion surveys conducted at the time would have corroborated this point.) Writing at the end of 1989, Popov warned that the political turmoil accompanying elections and the new habit of "taking to the streets" could provide fertile soil for "ideas of populism, egalitarianism, confiscation" (somewhat later he specified the danger as "left-wing populism"). In particular, Popov was concerned that such sentiments might be translated into the kind of legislation that could undo all the advantages of projected economic reforms, for example, arbitrary taxes on property or excessive social guarantees for low-income groups.

These warnings against the potentially negative consequences of egalitarianism and populism served to highlight the urgency of what Popov regarded as appropriate countermeasures, namely, accelerated denationalization and privatization of property. Here Popov appeared to share Migranian's general view (see chapter 3) that to be successful, the economic and political liberation of Soviet society had to proceed in a particular sequence and in properly balanced doses. Thus rational behavior in the political sphere would be encouraged to the extent that the individual was given the opportunity to think in terms of "*his* land, *his* business unit, *his* cooperative, *his* stock shares" (emphasis in original). Widespread identification with personal property in some form would function as at least a partial antidote to the principal "contradiction" of the reformist course, i.e., the tensions and grievances created by increased economic inequalities in the context of political democratization.

But there was also another, somewhat more ambiguous element in Popov's views on how to confront this "contradiction." It concerned his conception of the very nature of democracy and, in particular, the need to set certain limits to it. On the one hand, as noted earlier, he proclaimed his adherence to the principle that there could be no retreats, no "compromises," on the issue of democracy. But the same 1989 article that affirmed this principle also warned that "unlimited democracy" (as exemplified by the right of voters to influence directly the level of property taxes and social guarantees) could threaten the implementation of essential economic reforms. The democratization process was leaning excessively toward the enhancement of "representative" or legislative power; it needed increased reliance on responsible (and popularly elected) executive authority. By the following year there was a heightened sense of urgency to Popov's warnings about the inadequacy of "the purely democratic model" and the need to devise "institutions of political power that will depend less on populism" (compare Popov 1989 and 1990b). There was nothing in Popov's writings in 1989–90 that suggested a repudiation of the need for political democratization in some form, indeed for "unprecedented" democratization. But there was a real danger inherent in this process under Soviet circumstances, and, once again, its source was all too familiar: "Democracy, after all, always carries with it the danger that social justice will grow into leveling (*uravnitel'nost'*)" (1989).

Our review of Soviet discussions of economic inequality has sought to reveal some of the diversity of views on this issue in the Soviet literature in 1985–90. We have not attempted a comprehensive survey of these discussions but focused on those voices that most clearly reflected conflicting responses to this issue. The roughly equivalent attention paid above to these differing responses, however, should not obscure the fact that the dominant theme in these discussions was the criticism of wage and income leveling and the desirability of removing obstacles to increased economic inequalities. It may seem curious, but in this respect the dominant theme in 1985–90 was in essential continuity with the official position repeatedly reiterated during most of the period since Stalin launched his attack on egalitarianism in 1931.

However, the end of the 1980s witnessed some interesting changes in the way the critics of income leveling made their case. Readers will recall Lisichkin's example of the two adjoining farms with markedly differing levels of labor productivity but with essentially similar earnings' levels for the two groups of farm workers. This was a familiar type of illustration in the older antiegalitarian literature—differences in the intensity and skill of labor unaccompanied by comparable differentiation in labor income. Significantly, the more recent attacks on income leveling have invoked a somewhat different group of occupations to make their point. As noted earlier, the successful transition to a market-directed economy would require relatively high incomes for "intermediaries," those engaged in finance, trade, and entrepreneurial activities, including some groups whose incomes would derive primarily from property holdings. Thus the principal basis for income inequalities was no longer the familiar one—differences in the "quantity and quality of labor expended"—but the market's assessment of the relative value of the particular group's contribution to economic well-being.

In some respects, however, both the tone and the substance of the attacks on leveling have remained essentially unchanged. The unrestrained nature of these attacks, the unqualified denunciations elicited by suggestions to impose limits on income differentials and the inheritance of financial assets continued to have an almost frantic, emergency-like quality. The intensity of the anti-egalitarian response seemed strangely at odds with the relatively moderate nature of the proposals in the proegalitarian literature (we assume the writings of Rogovin are representative of the latter). There was no hint among the antilevelers that there may be some positive, "solidaristic" functions performed by placing limits on income inequalities. Their certainty that wider income differentiation would have a positive impact on economic performance was no less than that of "official" scholars in earlier decades who proclaimed that distribution in accordance with work in the present would pave the way for distribution in accordance with need sometime in the future. The apparent urgency of making the transition to a market system in the late 1980s obviously added to the vigor of the antiegalitarian current in these discussions. But it would have been interesting if the antilevelers (or levelers, for that matter) had confronted a related issue: Why should increased income inequality be so essential in the Soviet Union if Western empirical studies have found that some relatively efficient market economies (Sweden, the United Kingdom, and Japan) have income distributions that do not differ markedly from that of the Soviet Union?[4]

As the confrontation between the levelers and their opponents continued in 1989–90, the language of both groups began to reflect the particular combination of economic crisis and appeals for systemic reform that characterized those years. Thus, while some (Rogovin, 1989, p. 145) insisted that if society was now experiencing shortages, "every citizen must share them" (the point was made in the context of a demand that various systems of "privileges" must be eliminated), others conveyed a very different message (Volkonskii, 1990, p. 63) in warning that an effective economy required respect for those who know how to "make money." Clearly, the last thing that could be expected from the transition to a market system was that the issue of distributive justice would fade away.

Notes

1. This refers to the ratio of the wage exceeded by the 10 percent most highly paid workers to the wage below which are found the 10 percent lowest paid.

2. Discussing the influence of illegal incomes, Mikul'skii noted that the degree of differentiation of "aggregate" incomes (including those from illegal sources) was "much greater" than the differentiation of legal labor incomes and that any reasonable increase in the differentiation of the latter would not lead to the degree of inequality generated by the impact of illegal incomes on the overall distribution of income (1988, p. 12).

3. Unfortunately, neither Shokhin (1989) nor Kirichenko and Shmarov (1988) specify the income received by those they characterize as high-income (*vysokoobespechennye*) and low-income (*maloobespechennye*) groups. Perhaps the most frequently cited symbol of the preferential treatment accorded the former is that the prices paid for meat by low-income groups were approximately 50 percent higher than the prices available to the more well-to-do (see also Rimashevskaia, 1988, p. 6).

4. We refer to the studies of Abram Bergson as summarized by Gregory and Stuart, 1986, pp. 342–44.

5

The Desanctification of Marxism-Leninism

In one way or another the principal controversies reviewed thus far illustrate an obvious process of "escalation" that characterized Soviet public discourse on economic and political issues in the late 1980s. Whether the issue was workplace democratization, the legitimacy of political pluralism and a reassessment of "bourgeois" democracy, or appropriate grounds for inequalities in economic status, we may observe a growing readiness to transcend not only the views that prevailed in the pre-Gorbachev period but also those that represented the initial versions of the reformist position. By and large, however, the discussions that have concerned us up to this point were conducted within a "socialist" orientation and did not directly challenge the official Soviet version of Marxist-Leninist ideology. But while they did not explicitly call for the abandonment of this ideology, these discussions certainly helped prepare the groundwork for the direct ideological challenges that emerged at the end of the decade.

Our objective in this chapter is to examine some of the critical discussions that went well beyond those reviewed thus far in that they explicitly called into question traditional Soviet conceptions of socialism and the very foundations of Marxist-Leninist ideology. Of the outpouring of literature in 1988–90 that directly challenged what were formerly regarded as "sacred" truths, we consider a few examples that best illustrate the expansionary

logic of these discussions. For this purpose we focus on (a) the
controversies associated with the writings of A. Tsipko, and
(b) the confrontation between Soviet advocates of Western-style
social democracy and their opponents—mainly from the "right."
While the erosion of official state ideology was obviously a process that had long been under way,[1] the discussions reviewed
below demonstrate that the explicit repudiation of that ideology
had become fairly common in the Soviet literature by the late
1980s. Even the responses to its strongest critics reflected its
weakening hold.

Tsipko's Challenge: Stalinism and Marxism

Judging by the sheer volume as well as the content of published
reactions that they generated, a series of articles by A. Tsipko
(1988–89) played a decisive role in extending the boundaries of
what had already become relatively untrammeled (by Soviet
standards) political and intellectual discourse. The author was on
the editorial board of the country's leading sociological journal
and associated with the Institute of Economics of the World Socialist System, but the appearance of Tsipko's articles in a leading "popular science" journal rather than in an "academic"
publication undoubtedly enhanced their impact. The critical
theme repeatedly invoked by Tsipko was the need to identify the
"doctrinal" causes and sources of Stalinism, of "the practices of
the 1930s," and more generally of "our failures in socialist construction" (1988a, pp. 46, 47, 53). While a burgeoning literature
on the phenomenon of Stalinism had begun to emerge in the
more open Gorbachev period, it was precisely the studied failure
of these writings to confront what Tsipko regarded as the obvious
connection between Stalin's repressions and the "doctrine" or
ideology that inspired them that the author found so reprehensi-
ble. It was as though there were an invisible but rigid boundary
line that the critical literature on Stalinism refused to cross.
Tsipko was especially contemptuous of those who were prepared
to link the emergence of Stalin with the "patriarchal" values of

the Russian peasantry, but who completely ignored the connection between "Stalinist socialism" and the theoretical foundations of the revolutionary movement that brought the Bolsheviks to power. After all, was it not finally time "to begin at the beginning, to begin with the word"—the initial "doctrine"?

The challenging nature of Tsipko's discussion becomes apparent when we consider some of the explicit questions that his readers now confronted in a Soviet journal (the first of these questions he characterized as the "central" one). Was it possible to build a nonbarracks, democratic socialism on a nonmarket foundation? Can there be firm guarantees of personal freedom and democracy when the state is the only employer and people lack independent sources of subsistence? Does not the concept of a revolutionary vanguard lead to new forms of social inequality? What aspects of Marx's theory have been confirmed, what was applicable only to the nineteenth century, and in what respects were Marx and Engels mistaken? It would be difficult, indeed impossible, to demonstrate that Tsipko's own discussion represented anything like a systematic response to these questions. But the mere posing of these questions in a Soviet journal, and the particular manner in which they were formulated, constituted an argument: the need for a critical reappraisal of the Marxian intellectual heritage and the revolutionary movement it had inspired in the Soviet Union.

While such questions obviously transcended the issue of Stalinism, they provided the general context within which Tsipko elaborated his thesis concerning the organic link between Marxism and Stalinism. The urgency of recognizing such a link seemed all the greater now that the Soviet literature on the subject commonly sought to "expunge" Stalin from the history of Marxism and to demonstrate that the socialism built under his leadership had no relation to the socialism of Marx or even of Trotsky. In fact, argued Tsipko (1988a, p. 50), "as a whole, Stalin's views and conceptions of socialism were typical of Marxists" of his day. After all, Tsipko reminded his Soviet readers, Stalin developed as a personality in "a Marxist environment," assimilated the Marxist "classics" to the extent that his abilities permitted, and never went beyond the "elementary truisms of Marxism in his articles and speeches." Tsipko's relatively unqualified identification of Stalin's views with the "initial doctrine" was expressed with particular bluntness in his insistence that there were no essential differences between "the Marxist Stalin and the Marxist Kautsky" in their conceptions of the "ultimate goals" of a socialist economy. That is, both were guided by the vision of an economy in which profit maximization would be replaced by "nonmarket, noncommodity" forms of economic organization. The apparently common Marxian roots of Stalin's and Kautsky's conceptions of a socialist economy clearly seemed more significant to Tsipko (or at least more worthy of elaboration to a Soviet audience) than Kautsky's intense opposition to Bolshevism, and to Stalinist economic policies in particular.

It appeared obvious to Tsipko that it was precisely "Marx's model" of a socialist economy that Stalin and the earlier Bolshevik leadership adopted when they implemented their principal economic policies. Indeed, it was this model that could be held responsible for the disastrous record of Soviet economic and political history. "Imagine what would happen to our country if we made still another attempt, this time our third (after War Communism and Stalin's attack on the market), to build our economy in accordance with Marx's model, i.e., on the basis of direct product exchange and absolute directive planning from above" (1988a, p. 53).

Above all, argued Tsipko, it was in his intensely antipeasant attitudes and agricultural policies that Stalin most clearly displayed his essential continuity with the Bolshevik old guard and with the Marxian intellectual heritage (1988a, pp. 48, 52; 1988b, p. 44). Was it not obvious that Stalin's agricultural collectivization of the early 1930s was closely related to the "surplus appropriation system" (*prodrazverstka*) that constituted the very core of War Communism, the policies adopted by the Bolshevik leadership in the immediate postrevolutionary years? Stalin would not have received the support of the party for a policy of "expropriation of the countryside" (collectivization) unless he was able to justify it with what Tsipko characterized as "Marxist ideas." What were these ideas? On this issue Tsipko seemed to stretch matters a bit. Thus he noted that Stalin used the thesis of "the idiocy of rural life" (an expression invoked by Marx and Engels in *The Communist Manifesto*) to help make the case for collectivization. But Tsipko did not bother to add that when Marx and Engels used this expression, they did so in the context of demonstrating the positive consequences of the expansion of the bourgeoisie—one of which was the "rescue" of large portions of the population from the aforementioned "idiocy."[2]

However, Tsipko's argument concerning the role that "Marxist ideas" played in justifying Stalinist collectivization was not confined to this somewhat questionable illustration. Stalin ("like Trotsky," noted Tsipko) derived from Marxism the general notion of the incompatibility of small-scale, peasant production with a nonmarket socialism in which large-scale socialized production would displace all other forms of work organization. In his attack against the rightist opposition within the party in 1929, noted Tsipko, Stalin drew on "the Marxist view of the peasantry as the last capitalist class." Stalin presumably shared with most of the Bolshevik old guard the view that the market and capitalism were essentially inseparable. Hence, everything associated with the market, "and above all, the free peasant" (in Tsipko's formulation), was viewed as politically dangerous and a significant obstacle on the path to genuine socialism. The "class approach" common among the Bolshevik leadership (an approach clearly rooted in Marxian ideology) obviously contributed to this view and in this sense helped to justify the "implantation" of collectivization on a free peasantry.

Our primary concern here is not the validity of Tsipko's argument but the significance—in the Soviet intellectual environment of the late 1980s—of his repeated coupling of "Marxist ideas" with Stalinist policies. It was the striking novelty of this message (as an explicit argument in published form) that marked a turning point in Soviet discussions of this issue and generated some of the responses we examine below. The message, simply put, was that all the main features of Stalinism (including the mass repressions of the 1930s) and their continuing negative impact on Soviet life were not the result of departures from Marxian views and socialist principles but the product of policies intended to implement these views and principles. There was a peculiar irony inherent in this message that was surely not lost on some Soviet readers. During Stalin's lifetime, the need to link his policies with the sacred truths of Marxism was obligatory for all Soviet commentators on these matters, obviously as a means of justifying such policies. But to the extent that readers accepted Tsipko's case for the affinity between Stalinism and Marxism, the impact was surely to accelerate the discrediting of the latter and of the whole idea of socialism. Thus, what we referred to earlier as Tsipko's novel message was both novel and painfully familiar.

There was an additional element of irony in Tsipko's discussion that is worth noting. His characterization of some of the Bolshevik leaders executed under Stalin's rule was no less harsh—and in the case of Trotsky, even harsher—than his treatment of Stalin himself. Tsipko made it clear that he had no intention of absolving the "tyrant" of his crimes, but that the time had come to recognize that the "creations" of Stalinism could not be separated "from the general logic of the development of our revolution" (1988a, p. 48). Stalinism was not only the tragedy of the Bolshevik movement but also its "historical fault" (1989b, p. 53). It was the Bolshevik old guard, after all, that created the kind of political mechanism—the party as an "instrument of absolute rule"—that Stalin later used for his own purposes. Indeed, noted Tsipko, it was the old guard that, before Lenin's death, voluntarily turned over to Stalin the leadership of the party, together with the "boundless power" that the revolution had given it. Moreover, the process leading to the mass repressions of the 1930s had its beginnings well before Stalin's accession to power. It was in connection with their role in this process that Tsipko invoked the names of such Bolshevik leaders as Kamenev, Zinoviev, and Trotsky. While the "interests of the revolution" had long been regarded among leading Russian social democrats[3] as transcending democratic values, Trotsky carried this way of thinking a step further. He "placed the success of the revolution not only above the sovereignty of the people, of the majority, but also above the principles of universal human or normative morality" (Tsipko, 1988b, p. 43). Guided by the notion that "the revolution comes first," he sought to legitimize acts of repression (in some cases including execution) against opponents of the regime, even if the latter had recently been allies in the revolutionary cause. Trotsky and other Bolshevik leaders, in effect, helped adapt the Soviet population to the view that reprisals against political opponents were normal and justified measures. In this sense, the mass terror of Stalinism represented the culmination of a process that Stalin did not initiate. "If it was appropriate to use repression against Socialist Revolutionaries who had their own views about October, then why should it not be used against Bolshevik revolutionaries who insisted on their own ideas about how to build socialism?" (ibid., p. 43). Thus, among the principal sources of Stalinism, for Tsipko, were the traditions of "Russian left radicalism" (or "revolutionary maximalism"), traditions that were well represented in the early leadership of the Bolshevik regime.

The irony for Tsipko's readers was all too obvious and perhaps by now somewhat familiar. People characterized in Stalin's time as "spies," "wreckers," and "traitors" were indeed rather villainous historical figures, but their villainy consisted in their leadership of a revolutionary movement that must be regarded as responsible for the emergence of a Stalin.[4]

Responses to Tsipko and Escalation
of the Challenge

Perhaps the most striking quality of the bulk of the published reactions to Tsipko's articles was that they acknowledged the legitimacy of at least some of the questions and issues he posed. The unqualified defense of Marxism-Leninism that had been so common in the past was absent even in some of the most critical responses to Tsipko's arguments. Indeed, such critical responses commonly included an acknowledgment of the limitations of the Marxian intellectual heritage and serious "mistakes" by Lenin. Moreover, with the passage of time, we may detect a tendency toward a more positive assessment of Tsipko's writings, even within the successive articles of a particular commentator. What follows should help illustrate these propositions but is not intended as a comprehensive review of the responses to Tsipko's arguments.

Among the more critical responses was that of A.P. Butenko, a scholar at the Institute of Economics of the World Socialist System (1989a, 1989b). But before spelling out his criticism, Butenko made a point of stressing that he was in "full agreement" with Tsipko that it was altogether appropriate to confront the question of what there was in Marx's theory that had been confirmed, what was valid only for the nineteenth century, and what was mistaken. Like all mortals, Marx and Engels could hardly be expected to provide unambiguously correct answers to all questions they posed. In short, they "made mistakes," and such mistakes should be revealed and corrected. While Butenko's acknowledgment of this human quality in Marx and Engels can hardly strike Western readers as an earth-shattering discovery, it would be something of a challenge to establish the last time the same point had been made so explicitly in a Soviet publication.

However, Butenko's primary focus here was not on the errors of Marx and Engels but on those of Tsipko. Butenko explicitly rejected what he regarded as Tsipko's two principal—and obviously related—arguments.[5] The first of these, in Butenko's formulation, was the notion that "Stalin was a consistent Marxist-Leninist," that his policies were guided by the "theory of scientific socialism" (1989a, pp. 20–21). Could Tsipko be serious? wondered Butenko. Without undertaking a comprehensive response, Butenko focused on what appeared to him as the striking contrast between Lenin's "cooperative plan" for agriculture (formulated after the repudiation of War Communism) and Stalin's collectivization policy. The former was presumably intended as a long-term, gradual, and voluntary process of growth of genuine cooperatives, while the latter, with its reliance on coercion, expropriation, and mass repression, was obviously at odds with all the "basic Leninist principles" of agrarian policy (ibid., p. 23).

But it was the second of Tsipko's arguments (or "errors") that in some respects seemed more troublesome to Butenko, although it flowed logically from the first (which he dismissed rather casually). This was the view that the "barracks socialism" that emerged in the Soviet Union was the natural consequence of the political leadership's adherence to Marx's doctrine. For Butenko (1989b, p. 46) this was tantamount to placing the responsibility for Stalinism, with its mass repressions, on the shoulders of Karl Marx. Here Butenko recalled how Tsipko had sought to defend this conclusion. Had not Stalin ("like Trotsky") derived from Marx his view of the ultimate need to overcome commodity production (the market)? And—Tsipko's "central question"— was a nonbarracks, democratic socialism possible on a nonmarket foundation? Butenko's response followed (1989a, pp. 24–25; 1989b, p. 47). It was certainly true that Marx expected that the future postcapitalist society, with its highly developed "productive forces" (advanced technology), would rest on a "noncommodity" (nonmarket) foundation. But how could Marx and his vision of the future possibly be blamed for the fact that a political leadership began to destroy market relations prematurely, in a relatively underdeveloped economy? "Yes, Karl Marx, in assessing the objective trends of his time, thought that the course of history would increasingly undermine the objective foundations of value measurements, commodity–money relations, and a market and that all this would not exist in the future society. But Marx never recommended any such thing for Russia and the Bolsheviks" (Butenko, 1989b, p. 47).

However, in his eagerness to absolve Marx of any responsibility for the phenomenon of Stalinism,[6] Butenko appeared to go at least part of the way toward acknowledging that Stalin drew on some aspects of the Leninist heritage. What form did this partial concession to Tsipko take? Butenko admitted that if Tsipko had simply sought to demonstrate that the party program written by Lenin in 1919 (resting as it did on a "nonmarket and classless socialism") and the repressive policies of War Communism that were based on this program had played a significant role in promoting the kinds of "functionaries, . . . social institutions, and relations" on which Stalin would later draw to implant his barracks socialism, there would be no reason to dispute the point. However, Butenko was quick to remind his readers that the Leninist policies associated with War Communism (later allegedly repudiated by Lenin himself) could not be regarded as "direct antecedents" of Stalinism, since they were followed by the very different policies of the New Economic Policy (NEP). But in effect the damage was done. In the course of rejecting what appeared to him as Tsipko's principal arguments, Butenko acknowledged that the Leninist ideology and practices of the immediate postrevolutionary years were implicated in the impending rise of Stalinism.

In a subsequent article published at the end of 1989, and no longer directly concerned with responding to Tsipko's challenge, Butenko spelled out his conception of Lenin's "mistakes"—the word was used repeatedly by Butenko—during those years (1989c). The principal economic policies associated with War Communism (the appropriation of peasant surpluses, the "cavalry attacks on capital," the "statization" of almost all enterprises) could not be justified by the emergency conditions of the Civil War. These policies reflected a flawed vision of a "direct transition" to socialism in an underdeveloped country and indeed served to prolong the Civil War. While Lenin later admitted that the concept of a "direct transition to communist production and distribution" had proved mistaken, he failed to recognize what seemed to Butenko of supreme importance in the political sphere. Like any underdeveloped country that had not completed a "bourgeois-democratic transformation," postrevolutionary Russia urgently required "general democratic measures" that would create the "preconditions of civilization" (1989c, p. 41). When

Butenko characterized this failure on Lenin's part as a major error, he was making his own contribution to the ongoing process of desanctifying the Leninist heritage.[7]

Another critical response to Tsipko's challenge, accompanied by the critic's own explicit recognition of the failures of the Marxian vision, appeared in the writings of I. Kliamkin (1989). Although he largely rejected Tsipko's views, Kliamkin, like Butenko, acknowledged Tsipko's contribution in forcing the Soviet public to confront questions that had been essentially "blank spots" earlier—at least in the published literature. Thus it was no longer possible to ignore the theme of "Stalinism and Marxism," and it would be "absurd" to deny the legitimacy of Tsipko's question concerning the compatibility of a nonmarket system with a "nonbarracks, democratic socialism." What Kliamkin did deny, however, was what seemed to him the core of Tsipko's argument, namely, that the principal sources of Stalinism, its "doctrinal" roots, were to be found in Marx's conception of a nonmarket socialist society. For Kliamkin such "doctrinal" roots could not be regarded as a principal explanation for the emergence and functioning of Stalinism or any similar historical phenomenon. "Otherwise we would have to search in religious texts, for example, for the deepest source of all the complexities of the development of mankind in the Middle Ages" (Kliamkin, 1989, p. 42). Those who accepted Tsipko's view concerning the critical role of the nonmarket doctrine—Marx's "theoretical project"—as a principal source of Stalinism would have to confront some difficult questions. For example, how could one explain why such important figures as Plekhanov, Martov, and Kautsky, all of whom accepted the Marxian nonmarket project, rejected the Bolshevik revolution and regarded the Bolsheviks as having deviated from Marxism? Even more important, how could Tsipko's stress on the critical role of the doctrine of nonmarket socialism be reconciled with the fact that this "general plan," which was designed for economically developed Western countries and accepted by all major trends in the European social-democratic movement, "remained on paper" in these countries but was implemented in a country like Russia—for which it was certainly not intended?

Kliamkin's point in posing these questions, particularly the second one, was fairly clear. A given doctrine, associated with such different attitudes among its adherents and such different consequences in different countries, could hardly be held responsible for a social phenomenon like Stalinism. Tsipko's invocation of Marx's nonmarket "project" in this context was a substitute for historical analysis. The real challenge was to explain the differing fate of the same doctrine—Marx's nonmarket "project"—in different societies; in Kliamkin's formulation: How was Marxism transformed into Stalinism? What seems most significant about Kliamkin's response, which was simultaneously intended as a critique of Tsipko's argument, was that it was in no significant sense an old-style defense of the Marxian vision or of the policies of the Bolshevik old guard.

Briefly put, Kliamkin's response to his own formulation of these issues came to the following (ibid., pp. 48–50). The "Marxist project" was regarded by its founders as applicable to the developed countries of the West. Nonmarket socialism would emerge as a result of the ultimate exhaustion of the productive potential of the capitalist economy. But Marx and Engels clearly overestimated the probability of the "self-transcendence and self-exhaustion" of private property. In projecting their vision of a revolutionary transition to a postcapitalist society, Marx and Engels drew on the "real contradictions" and sharp class conflict that characterized early industrial capitalism. However, the continued expansion of the system permitted the Western bourgeoisie to reduce the intensity of these conflicts and to achieve the "economic and political integrations of the working class into the capitalist system." Thus the class on which Marx and Engels had pinned their hopes for a breakthrough to a nonmarket socialism obviously had not achieved the historical mission the founders of Marxism had assigned to it. Moreover, that class, along with the technology associated with it, was now leaving the historical stage, and there were no obvious grounds on which to expect its successors to come any closer to realizing the "Marxist project."

Kliamkin's account was obviously intended to stress the contrasting capacity of Western capitalism and the czarist regime to defuse the revolutionary potential of the socialist doctrine. While Western capitalism was able to "integrate" its working class, the opposite was the case in prerevolutionary Russia, where the continuing underdevelopment of the economy and political system aggravated class conflict and intensified both anticzarist and antibourgeois sentiments. "Social conflict, which in the West became a thing of the past, matured with catastrophic rapidity in Russia, and neither czarism nor the Russian bourgeoisie—as the eight months between February and October 1917 showed—could solve it" (ibid., p. 48). Under these circumstances, argued Kliamkin, the "tragedy and tragic fault" of the Bolshevik old guard was not the seizure of power but that, having seized power, they attempted (during War Communism) to apply the Marxist project of a postcapitalist, nonmarket socialist system in what was largely a precapitalist Russia. Nothing of the kind had been anticipated or provided for in the original Marxian doctrine. Nor did the doctrine provide any justification for repressive measures by a state apparatus in the new society, since such an apparatus presumably would be unnecessary with the anticipated elimination of class antagonism. However strange it may seem, the abandonment of War Communism and the introduction of NEP represented for Kliamkin "a return to the historical conception of Marx." In what sense? NEP policies were an attempt to create "the missing preconditions for civilized development," which Russia had failed to attain prior to the revolution, but which successful capitalist development had created in the West.

Thus Kliamkin's response to Tsipko was in no significant sense a defense of the validity of Marxian doctrine for either the West or Russia. But it was an attempt to absolve the doctrine of responsibility for the Soviet regime's pre-Stalinist repressive features and for the failed economic policies of War Communism, as well as for the phenomenon of Stalinism itself. What followed NEP, in Kliamkin's view, could be regarded as a "second edition" of War Communism.

But the implementation of Stalinist economic policies (forced industrialization and "barbaric" collectivization) required certain ideological preconditions in the form of a "correction of classical Marxism," or the "transformation of Marxism into Stalinism." For Kliamkin this process was most clearly embodied in the Stalinist thesis of a sharpening class struggle as the country moved closer to the attainment of socialism, the related conception of a "permanent civil war" (under conditions of civil peace), and the image of an omnipresent mass-produced "internal enemy." In its most concise version, then, the substance of Kliamkin's response to Tsipko's challenge might be formulated as follows: Whatever the variety of sources of Stalinism, this phenomenon was surely more closely associated with the above "corrections" of Marxism than with the original doctrine. The latter, with its nonmarket "project," was intended for a very different kind of society.

A somewhat more sympathetic reaction to Tsipko's writings appeared in some of the philosophical literature in 1989–90. But just as Tsipko's critics did not rest their case on an uncritical reaffirmation of Marxism-Leninism, Tsipko's defenders—or at least those whose views we consider briefly below—did not rely on a simplistic identification of Stalinism with Marxism. An article by A.F. Kolodii (1989) in one of the country's leading philosophical journals illustrates the kind of positive response to Tsipko we have in mind. Kolodii declared his readiness "to support and, to a certain degree, to develop" the ideas of Tsipko on the "doctrinal preconditions" of the Stalinist years (ibid., p. 61). This did not prevent him from explicitly acknowledging that Stalin obviously "distorted Marxism," among other ways by departing from its "humanistic spirit," by substituting means for ends, and by attempting to transform Marxism into a set of "indisputable truths." But after all, Stalinism represented more than the views of a particular individual. This was a phenomenon that arose within one of the mainstreams of the international working-class movement, and it was perfectly legitimate to pose the issue of the doctrinal sources of Stalinism.

Kolodii's partial support for Tsipko's position took the form of elaborating the theme of the "internal contradictions" of the Marxian doctrine. This concept was repeatedly invoked by Kolodii to demonstrate the conflict ("contradiction") between what appeared to him as the scientific elements of the doctrine on the one hand and the ideological form of the doctrine on the other—its use as "a weapon in the class struggle." What concerns us here is the manner in which Kolodii sought to illustrate these two integral components of the doctrine—science and ideology—and to suggest a link between its ideological form and Stalinism (ibid., pp. 65, 67–68). As illustrative of the "scientific character" of Marxism, Kolodii cited the following: the recognition by the founders of the doctrine that it was impossible to provide anything like a blueprint of the future socialist society or the precise path of transition to it, a readiness to search for the most appropriate forms of socialism given the particular circumstances of the country (exemplified by Lenin's transition to NEP in 1921), and a general "openness to new facts and ideas." But in other contexts, and no less frequently, the same doctrine revealed its negative qualities as an "ideological weapon." As illustrations of this aspect of the doctrine, Kolodii invoked the following: an exaggerated conception of the degree to which Marxism (Marxist "social science") had discovered the "laws" governing social change; the belief that basic social transformations invariably require "the violent destruction of prevailing relations"; an "irreconcilable attitude" to any versions of non-Marxian, petty-bourgeois socialism, or—the same point formulated somewhat differently—a strict orientation to "pure" and "uncompromising" proletarian socialism. These and similar views reflected an abiding ideological intolerance, a sense of "irreconcilable differences" with political opponents and adherents of alternative doctrines that was characteristic of Marxism from the very beginning. But, insisted Kolodii, while in the pre-Stalinist years these ideological components coexisted with humanistic and scientific elements of the doctrine cited above and a readiness to admit mistakes (here Kolodii cited Lenin and his ability to learn from "practice"), under Stalinism the principle of "irreconcilability" (*neprimirimost´*) became virtually the only distinctive element of the doctrine. The treatment of this principle as an "absolute," when joined to the "class approach" long associated with Marxism, contributed significantly to what Kolodii characterized as the completely unjustified brutalities of the Stalinist epoch.

Thus the grounds for Kolodii's explicit support for some of Tsipko's principal theses were clear: Whatever Stalin's distortions of Marxism, Stalinism also drew on significant elements of the Marxian heritage. As for the lessons to be drawn from all this, the issue, at least for Kolodii, was not the need to abandon socialist values. Rather, what was urgently required was the replacement of the familiar cultlike (*kul´tovyi*) attitude toward the Marxian doctrine by a "constructively critical" one. Kolodii did not spell out precisely what this implied, but one of its positive consequences would be a more realistic approach to the limits of "social engineering" (ibid., p. 68).

An additional illustration—the last we shall consider—of a generally sympathetic response to the issues raised by Tsipko appeared in an article by the philosopher A. Nikiforov (1990). Although Nikiforov's discussion made only a passing but distinctly favorable reference to Tsipko's writings, it was closer in spirit to the latter than any of the commentaries discussed immediately above. This is hardly surprising. The responses of Butenko, Kliamkin, and Kolodii to Tsipko's challenge all appeared in 1989. With the passage of time (Nikiforov's article appeared in mid-1990), explicitly critical assessments of the Marxian intellectual heritage became increasingly common.

As a specialist in philosophy, Nikiforov focused his discussion on the fate of Marxist philosophy in the postrevolutionary period, particularly during the years of Stalinist rule. But it was clear from the context of his discussion that his remarks on the fate of philosophy were no less applicable to other spheres of intellectual activity and to any efforts at independent thinking. This is a point worth keeping in mind in the remarks that follow. Nikiforov's discussion rested largely on his elaboration of the concept of "the politization of Marxism," a process that arose early in the history of Marxism and that assumed ever more destructive forms until it culminated in Stalinism.[8] Well before the Soviet revolution, noted Nikiforov, some Marxists commonly regarded intellectual and philosophical disagreements between themselves and their opponents as necessarily reflecting conflicting political positions. This was especially characteristic of Lenin, "who did not recognize purely theoretical disagreements" and who regarded any departure from the views of Marx and Engels on philosophical issues as "a concession to bourgeois ideology that brought harm to the revolutionary struggle of the working class" (ibid., p. 116). Nikiforov pointed to the difference between Engels's *Anti-Dühring* and Lenin's *Materialism and Empirio-Criticism* as an indicator of the movement of Marxism "along the path of equating philosophical disputes with political disagreements." For Nikiforov the dominant orientation of some Marxists (obviously including Lenin) to "victory in the political struggle" rather than to the search for truth was a principal source of the extreme intolerance they often exhibited toward other philosophical traditions.

The "politization of Marxism" and the spirit of intolerance associated with it were intensified following victory in the revolution. It was as though that victory and the Bolsheviks' retention of power had shown that the Marxist doctrine was a "demonstrable truth," which only accomplices of the old exploiting classes could continue to deny. Groups that were formerly recognized as philosophical opponents were thus transformed into representatives of the "class enemy" (ibid., p. 118) and treated accordingly, that is, forced into exile or subjected to domestic political repression. But the point repeatedly invoked by Nikiforov was that this process of "politization" of the original doctrine, which reached unprecedented and deadly proportions during the years of Stalinism, drew on "elements that were characteristic of Marxism even in the prerevolutionary period" (ibid., p. 121).

Nikiforov did not deny the partial validity of the criticisms directed at Tsipko to the effect that the latter ignored the fundamental differences between "genuine" Marxism and Stalinism. There was a considerable element of truth in such criticisms, but "not the whole truth." Surely it was time to recognize that not every philosophical doctrine could lend itself to transformation into a "state myth" and serve as a justification for political and intellectual repression. What was there in Marxism (in "Marxist philosophy," as Nikiforov put it) that adapted it to this role and permitted Stalin to use it as an "ideological intoxicant"? Nikiforov's response appeared to go to the very core of the doctrine: "It was first of all the *dialectic*, which by means of its metaphors was able to explain anything and everything and readily lent itself to sophistry; it was the *class approach*, which in the moral sphere could imperceptibly be transformed into an absence of principles and a moral relativism; and perhaps most fundamentally, it was the *eschatological faith* of Marxism in a radiant future, for the sake of which any deprivation and crimes were justified" (ibid., p. 123).

This was precisely the kind of assessment, of course, that appeared to support Tsipko's thesis of the links between Marxism and Stalinism. But especially intriguing was the manner in which Nikiforov combined this view of the role of Marxism in the Soviet context with a very different assessment of its impact on the capitalist world, where he regarded it as having contributed to the democratization of capitalist society. Unfortunately, Nikiforov only hinted at but did not develop this theme of the complete reversal of Marxism's impact depending upon whether its adherents were in power or out of power. As for the doctrine's future prospects, Nikiforov was unambiguous (ibid., p. 128): "Too much in Marxist philosophy belongs to the nineteenth century."

Clearly, the issues raised by Tsipko concerning the doctrinal roots of Stalinism had an immediate catalytic impact on Soviet discussions of Marxism. The comparatively free-wheeling nature of the responses reviewed above, whether by Tsipko's critics or by his supporters, illustrate the process of desanctification of what had long been a sacred doctrine immune to explicit criticism.[9] But a similar process may also be observed in Soviet discussions in 1988–90 of issues that were quite distinct from those posed by Tsipko. In particular, some of the Soviet literature on Western capitalist societies both reflected and contributed to the erosion of the traditional doctrine. Of special interest is the role that the conflicting perspectives of social democracy and neoconservatism played in the desanctification of Soviet Marxism.

Social Democracy and Economic Liberalism

It will become apparent below that there was a considerable diversity of views in the Soviet literature of the late 1980s on developed capitalist economies. Our initial concern here is with those writings that simultaneously represented a departure from familiar Marxian characterizations of these economies and a sympathetic treatment of social-democratic views and policies. While this general orientation obviously emerged earlier, it was not until the end of the 1980s that it could be expressed in unambiguous and explicit form.

A clear illustration appeared in a 1988 article by V. Sheinis (1988a) in a monthly journal published by the country's leading research institute specializing in the study of foreign economies—the Institute of World Economy and International Relations. Sheinis appealed for the abandonment of certain basic propositions that continued to function as "sacred cows," blocking a realistic assessment of modern capitalism. In particular, he cited the continuing affirmation of such concepts as the decay and "general crisis" of capitalism and the view that the transition from capitalism to socialism represented the "basic content of the modern epoch." Surely the time had come to recognize that capitalism had been able to incorporate certain "economic and social stabilizers" that for decades had protected it against the kind of crises that could lead to its collapse. Moreover, Marx's expectation that with capitalist development the "accumulation of wealth at one pole" would be accompanied by the "accumulation of misery, agony of toil, slavery, ignorance . . . at the opposite pole" turned out to have some validity—in Sheinis's view—only at

early stages of capitalism. In highly developed bourgeois societies, such phenomena appear "only in exceptional circumstances
and in marginal spheres" (ibid., p. 13). It seemed obvious to
Sheinis that the capitalism described by Marx had been profoundly transformed through its ability to assimilate "collectivist
elements" (for example, "social guarantees, . . . public consumption funds, a developed system of cooperatives, consumers' societies") and that the social-democratic movement had played a
significant role in this transformation. Western capitalism had by
no means been transformed into socialism, but it certainly had
demonstrated an ability to incorporate institutional features originally associated with socialist doctrine; and although its model of
political democracy was "far from ideal," in this respect, too, it
had advanced well beyond the level attained during capitalism's
earlier stage of "free competition" (ibid., p. 14; Sheinis, 1988b, p.
25). Through its ability to combine the principles of "plan" and
"market," modern capitalism had become "a more or less adequate form of functioning and development of scientific-industrial
productive forces." Perhaps most challenging was Sheinis's formulation of the implications of all this for what was still official
state ideology. Simply freeing the "classical heritage" (Marxism-
Leninism) from the "vulgarizations" of recent years would no
longer do. Something much more fundamental was now
needed—a "new general theoretical paradigm" (Sheinis, 1988a,
pp. 5, 23).

It is worth noting that Sheinis's discussion reviewed above
appeared at approximately the same time (the end of 1988) as
Tsipko's initial articles on the doctrinal roots of Stalinism. Although the latter's writings obviously had a substantially greater
impact on Soviet public consciousness than the former's, both
operated in the same direction, that is, they both served to discredit the guiding doctrine of Marxism. Given the profound
changes in capitalism stressed in Sheinis's writings, had not the
"revolutionary transformation" of the system called for in the
Marxian doctrine become largely irrelevant, at least in the more
developed capitalist economies? But the consequences attributed

to the Marxian socialist doctrine—albeit in its transformed version of modern social democracy—were strikingly different for Sheinis than they were for Tsipko. For the former, capitalism had been "ennobled" by its ability to incorporate socialist elements in response to the pressures of the social-democratic movement (Sheinis, 1988b, p. 25). For Tsipko, as noted earlier, there was an essential continuity between some elements of the Marxian socialist doctrine and the phenomenon of Stalinism.

What was the relevance of the social-democratic movement, its ideology and experience, to the problems confronting Soviet society in the late 1980s in the midst of *perestroika*? This was a question explicitly posed in some of the Soviet literature of this period. The responses to this question, as well as related discussions that we briefly examine below, provided an unusual opportunity for a comparatively sympathetic portrayal of social-democratic views to receive a hearing in some Soviet publications.

Perhaps the clearest illustration of such an approach may be found in the writings of B.S. Orlov. European social democracy, noted Orlov, had steadily moved away from the view that socialism should be identified with the socialization or nationalization of the means of production. Given the search for more effective forms of economic organization in the Soviet Union, there was every reason to consider seriously the notion of a "mixed economy," which had come to be increasingly accepted by Western social democrats (Orlov, 1988, p. 128). What was critical in this view was not the extent of state ownership of productive property but the opportunity for workers to participate in determining "the conditions of their own work and pay" and the readiness of the state to redistribute profits through progressive taxation to meet the needs of society. Orlov noted that such functions could be performed within the framework of a variety of forms of property, including private, public, and cooperative, although social democrats had placed special emphasis on extending worker participation in ownership (as well as in management). What was clear to social democrats was the negative lesson to be learned from the Soviet experience: comprehensive socialization under the control of a state bureaucracy results in a "statization that has nothing in common with socialism" (1989, pp. 63–64).

Orlov also appealed for a careful study of social democrats' views on the market mechanism and their extensive experience in administering such an economy. Given Soviet economists' absorption with devising reform programs for their own economy, it was certainly worth knowing that social democrats had come to regard the market as an "irreplaceable" mechanism that effectively—without a huge state bureaucracy—coordinated a vast number of economic decisions, encouraged efficiency, and facilitated "structural changes" in response to changes in consumer demand (1988, p. 129; 1989, p. 64). But considering the unrestrained enthusiasm of some Soviet economists for the market, it was also worth stressing that social democrats recognized the "dark sides" of the market and did not accept its results as sacred (*ne moliatsia na rynok*) (1989, p. 64; 1990b, p. 25). In particular, social democrats were perfectly aware that the market, "by itself," could readily result in business cycles and unemployment, an unjust distribution of income, and damage to the environment. Hence the need for the "social correction of the market mechanism" through a variety of welfare-state policies. Indeed, for Orlov the welfare state, with its comparatively generous social benefits (especially in such countries as Sweden and Austria, where the influence of social democrats had long been dominant), was the social democrats' "main contribution to the development of world civilization" (1988, p. 130).

An additional aspect of this highly sympathetic characterization of social democracy is worth noting. Among the most important qualities of this movement, according to Orlov, was its commitment to the extension of democratic principles to all spheres of public life—economic, political, and social. Indeed, the principal goal or "destiny" of socialism was the "all-round development of democracy," a goal that—in the social-democratic view—Communists had repeatedly betrayed (ibid., p. 127). Nor was there anything in Orlov's exposition to suggest that this view was unwarranted. As for the social democrats' contribution to democratic institutions, the literature under review here illustrated this in two principal ways. First, in the political arena, social democrats had contributed to the emergence of a system that deserved the label of "representative democracy" rather than "bourgeois democracy." Their contribution took the form of a consistent struggle for universal suffrage, for the right to unrestricted organization of political parties, and for "freedom of political activity" (Orlov, 1989, pp. 64–65; Peregudov, 1990, p. 6). The larger significance of the social-democratic impact on capitalist political institutions was clearly formulated by Peregudov (1990, p. 7): "Adherence to the principles and norms of political democracy is a cornerstone of the ideology and political credo of social democracy. And the fact that the basic norms and principles of parliamentary democracy have now acquired the character of generally recognized values clearly confirms the ability of the social democrats to stimulate and accelerate profound qualitative changes in the whole system of social relations of capitalism. to transform capitalism from 'within.' "

Whatever the intentions of the author, Soviet readers could hardly be blamed for regarding such assessments of social democracy as, at the very least, an implicit argument in favor of assimilating the values of this movement and thus promoting the democratization of Soviet political life. Similarly, some of the Soviet literature linking the social-democratic movement with industrial (or economic) democracy had obvious implications for the reform of Soviet worker–management relations. Western social democrats were portrayed in these writings as closely associated with, often as leaders of, trade unions whose activities ranged from ordinary bargaining over wages and working conditions to more ambitious efforts to implement worker participation in management. The concept of industrial democracy was applied to the whole range of such activities (Orlov, 1988, p. 129). But especially significant was the contrasting picture that some of the literature reflecting a social-democratic orientation presented of Soviet trade unions and unions in some capitalist countries, particularly those in countries with "more or less developed democratic traditions" (Veber, 1988, p. 60). Soviet unions had typically functioned as "silent appendages" of management, and any meaningful forms of industrial democracy had long been largely inoperative. In some capitalist countries, however, unions functioned as the "collective voice" of employed workers, providing channels for the exercise of "democratic pressures" on management and, according to at least some empirical studies,[10] contributing to the improved productive performance of union plants (ibid., pp. 58–60). The implications of all this for reform of Soviet worker–management relations seemed more than obvious. The "democratization of production" through the encouragement of the kinds of unions that would simultaneously function as partners and opponents of management, a policy traditionally associated with social democracy, was clearly on the order of the day.

Finally, quite apart from the implications of social democracy for reform of the Soviet system, this movement (in Orlov's view) had so transformed capitalism that some of Marx's critical concepts were now of questionable validity. In particular, given the profound changes in worker–management relations introduced as a result of the joint efforts of social democracy and trade unions, Marx's concept of the "exploitation" of labor under capitalism seemed largely outdated—at least in some capitalist countries. But it clearly continued to be applicable to the Soviet Union (Orlov, 1990a, pp. 18–19; 1990b, p. 24).

As for the critical responses to social-democratic views in these years, perhaps their most striking quality was the prominent role that neoconservative ideology (or economic liberalism) in its Soviet version played in such responses. This is not to say that Marxist-Leninist orthodoxy was altogether silent in the face of some of the explicitly sympathetic characterizations of social democracy reviewed above. But the criticisms directed at social democracy in the name of Marxism-Leninism seemed almost perfunctory ("capitalism, although it has changed, has not ceased to be capitalism"),[11] and certainly less novel and less interesting than those reflecting neoconservative views. The beginnings of an open confrontation between Soviet economic liberalism (we use this term as a synonym for neoconservatism) and Soviet social democracy was itself a reflection of the declining relevance of traditional Marxist-Leninist ideology in the intellectual environment of the late 1980s. What follows is not intended as a comprehensive review of Soviet neoconservative thinking but will focus on the principal criticisms that adherents of this intellectual current directed against views commonly associated with social democracy.

Perhaps the sharpest attack on social democracy from the "right"[12] was embodied in Piiasheva's appeal (cited in chapter 3) to heed Hayek's warning that "even a peaceful, social-democratic road to socialism leads to . . . the suppression of individualism, democracy, and individual freedom." However, neither Piiasheva (1989) nor other Soviet critics of social democracy (for example, Pinsker, 1989) provided explicit justification for such doomsday warnings. The case for linking social democracy with the suppression of individual freedom appeared to rest (implicitly) on the critics' portrayal of the substantial role that state intervention in the economy played in this movement's ideology and policies. Surely, Piiasheva seemed to imply, the extensive direction of economic activity by state authorities carried with it the inherent danger of the suppression of political and personal freedom.

But whatever the ultimate implications of interventionist policies for personal freedom, the bulk of the Soviet neoconservative criticism of Western social democracy centered on its allegedly disastrous economic consequences. Here is Pinsker's characterization of these consequences (1989, p. 187): "In the mid-1970s the old verdict concerning the deepening general crisis of capitalism became justified. However, the crisis was by no means generated by the anarchy of competition but by the growth of state expenditures and the increasing role of the state in social and economic life." What were the principal economic policies that such critics of social democracy and the welfare state found particularly damaging?

Perhaps the major target of the neoconservative critics was the social democrats' absorption with the problem of guaranteeing economic stability, or "ending the cyclical character of development of the capitalist market economy" (Piiasheva, 1989, p. 98). It was in the name of this supreme goal that social democrats continually sought to implement policies that would ensure full employment, steady economic growth (at a rate sufficient to maintain full employment), and stable prices. What they did not seem to realize, in the view of such critics as Pinsker (1989, p. 184) and Piiasheva (1989, p. 96), was that declines in aggregate demand were an integral and potentially healthy aspect of the market mechanism, that they had a "positive economic meaning." Cyclical downturns eliminated firms and industries operating at a loss (thereby raising labor productivity), promoted the scrapping of obsolete equipment, and released investment resources and labor surpluses for employment in more profitable, expanding sectors. Unfortunately, social-democratic policies damaged this normal adjustment mechanism ("the rules of the market game") by increasing government spending (to offset declines in aggregate demand), incurring budgetary deficits and subsidizing obsolete sectors—all in the interests of economic stability and full employment. The consequences of the expanding economic role of the state, particularly during periods of social-democratic (or labor-party) rule, seemed unambiguous to Pinsker (1989, p. 193): "State stimulation of the economy, as a rule, pumps capital from the more productive, which means the more promising and more profitable, branches to the less productive branches, demoralizing industrialists and reducing the competitiveness of the national economy. By rewarding the weak and punishing the strong, the bureaucrat preserves unprofitability at one pole and simultaneously undermines the possibility of growth at the other."

Similarly dysfunctional and counterproductive, in this view, were some of the principal institutional mechanisms incorporated in the welfare state in response to pressures from "reformist advocates of equality and redistribution" (Pinsker, 1989, pp. 188, 194, 199–200). Through its excessive "public charity," the welfare state tended to demoralize and weaken the poor, thereby blocking their "path upward" (here Pinsker relied on the work of the "eminent American economist" George Gilder). Redistributive policies that reduced income inequalities by transferring incomes from the more diligent and skilled members of the working population to those whose low wages sometimes reflected their "laziness, incompetence, and unwillingness to learn" could not help but reduce work incentives. Pinsker's formulation here was obviously the analogue to his characterization of the process of subsidizing noncompetitive and low-profitability firms out of "con- fiscatory" taxes levied on the more profitable sectors—"rewarding the weak and punishing the strong."

These highly critical assessments of social democracy and the welfare state (accompanied by a distinctly negative attitude toward the role of trade unions)[13] were naturally presented in the context of commentaries on capitalist economies. But their authors—Soviet adherents of economic liberalism—were obviously concerned with stressing their relevance to the task of transforming the Soviet system. Surely it would be a mistake to "borrow the errors" of the social democrats. Or, formulating the same issue in somewhat different terms: "Cannot we use Milton Friedman's or Friedrich Hayek's ideas?" (Piiasheva, 1989, pp. 99, 136).

Whatever the comprehensive answer that Soviet neoconservatives would ultimately give to this question, it was already clear from their writings of the late 1980s that their conception of a reformed Soviet economy and society rested on the acceptance of the following general principles: (a) the primacy of the "values of economic, political, and social freedom," (b) a dominant role for private ownership of property (by 1990 this had escalated to "full"—*polnyi*—privatization) as a necessary "material foundation" for political democracy and an efficient economy, and (c) a minimalist state "subordinate to the principles of liberalism," whose functions would be largely confined to "responsibility for the enforcement of laws" (Pinsker, 1989, pp. 201–2; Seliunin, 1989, p. 212; Piiasheva, 1990, p. 79).

Once again it must be stressed that the Soviet literature on social democracy and neoconservatism reviewed here (as well as the discussion generated by Tsipko's articles) reflected the initial opportunities that critics of official doctrine had for the comparatively open expression of their views. Moreover, these markedly unconventional views (to put it mildly) appeared within the institutional framework of a society whose economic resources—including those required to publish these views—remained largely under state and party control. Certainly no extensive "privatization" had yet emerged. But even at this early stage, on the threshold of the 1990s, it seemed clear that opposition ideologies were in the process of seriously challenging what had long been sacred doctrine. The erosion of the latter, even within the ruling party, had become all too obvious. What remained unclear was whether any ideologies other than some version of social democracy and neoconservatism—in particular, more "leftist" or "radical" ideologies—could continue as serious contenders in the political and intellectual arena. But surely, whatever new movements might emerge, or whatever new forms old movements might take, it seemed almost inconceivable that they would rely on the familiar combination of basic principles: comprehensive state ownership of productive property, a constitutionally enshrined "leading role" for a single political party, and a world view guided by textbook Marxism-Leninism.

Notes

1. Some dissident literature of the 1970s argued that the official ideology had long since ceased to be taken seriously by most Soviet citizens. See Kolakowski, 1977, p. 289.

2. See Tucker, 1978, p. 477.

3. Tsipko cited the writings of the Russian Marxist G.V. Plekhanov in this connection (1988b, p. 43).

4. Tsipko did not explicitly link Lenin to the emergence of Stalin or the latter's policies, at least in the writings discussed in this section.

5. It should be noted that Butenko's articles reviewed here were obviously submitted for publication following the appearance of only one or two of Tsipko's four articles on the sources of Stalinism.

6. Thus Butenko insisted (1989b, p. 48), with some justification, that there were no grounds for Tsipko's charge that "Marx's model" of the future society rested on "absolute directive planning from above." Such characterizations of Marx's views amounted to "Stalinizing" Marxism.

7. Butenko (1989c, p. 43) also admitted that there were acts of "mass terror and brutality" during the early years of Bolshevik rule under Lenin's leadership but noted that they had occurred in the context of "the brutality of enemies of the revolution." Moreover, insisted Butenko, violence for Lenin was not "an end in itself," and he never used it for the purpose of enhancing his personal power—presumably by contrast with Stalin.

8. Nikiforov's "politization of Marxism" was obviously analogous in some respects to Kolodii's theme of the "internal contradictions of Marxism." Both pointed to the pre-Stalinist roots of policies pursued in the 1930s.

9. A fuller account of Tsipko's own contribution to this process, which we do not undertake here, would have to take account of his writings in 1990. Early that year (Tsipko, 1990a, p. 83) he declared: "There are more than sufficient grounds for a serious, critical attitude to everything that Karl Marx wrote." For his attempt to apply this principle, see Tsipko, 1990b. An interesting illustration of how the desanctification of Marxism may be accompanied by the sanctification of another doctrine is suggested by Tsipko's remark in the latter source (p. 203) that "nothing so develops thought, the soul, and the heart as the search for God."

10. Veber (1988, p. 63) draws here on the work of U.S. economists Richard Freeman and James Medoff.

11. Vaziulin, 1988, p. 27.

12. The "right" is used here in its traditional Western sense to refer to views sympathetic to minimum state intervention in the economy.

13. "Trade unions and other social and cooperative organizations, occupying a significant role in the life of modern societies and once regarded as a mode of protecting the weak individual from the pressures of powerful market forces and the arbitrariness of the bureaucracy, have become bureaucratized as they have grown stronger and larger and oppress the citizen no less than any other monopoly" (Pinsker, 1989, p. 200). Trade unions were a prime example of "group egoism" for Pinsker.

BIBLIOGRAPHY

Akademiia nauk SSSR, Institut sotsiologicheskikh issledovanii; Sovetskaia sotsiologicheskaia assotsiatsiia (1982). *Sotsial'naia spravedlivost' i puti ee realizatsii v sotsial'noi politike*. Moscow: Institut sotsiologicheskikh issledovanii AN SSSR.

——— (1984). *Sotsial'nye aspekty raspredelitel'noi politiki*. Moscow: Institut sotsiologicheskikh issledovanii AN SSSR.

Alekseev, A., and Maksimov, B. (1988). "Expand the Sphere of Direct Self-Management." *Sotsialisticheskii trud*, no. 10, pp. 19–24.

Ambartsumov, E. (1988). "On Means of Improving the Political System of Socialism." In Iu.N. Afanas'ev, ed., *Inogo ne dano*, pp. 77–96. Moscow: Progress.

Amelin, V. (1989). "Informals, Intelligentsia, Party Activists: Political Orientations." *Obshchestvennye nauki*, no. 4, pp. 199–217.

——— (1990). "From the Dictates of the Bureaucracy to a Political Market." *Obshchestvennye nauki*, no. 1, pp. 96–108.

Artemev, S., and Illarionov, V. (1987). "The Management of Labor on a Scientific Basis." *Sotsialisticheskii trud*, no. 6, pp. 62–75.

Åslund, A. (1989). *Gorbachev's Struggle for Economic Reform*. Ithaca: Cornell University Press.

Auzan, A. (1989). "Contradictions in the Process of Development of Self-Management." *Sotsialisticheskii trud*, no. 7, pp. 41–46.

Barabasheva, N.S., and Vengerov, A.B. (1988). *Pravo i raspredelenie*. Moscow: Izdatel'stvo Moskovskogo universiteta.

Batkin, L. (1989). "The Dead Seizes the Living." *Literaturnaia gazeta*, September 20.

Blium, R.N. (1987). "Alienation and Socialism." *Filosofskie nauki*, no. 9, pp. 112–14. English translation in *Soviet Studies in Philosophy*, vol. 27, no. 2.

Butenko, A.P. (1989a). "Is Karl Marx to Blame for 'Barracks Socialism'?" *Filosofskie nauki*, no. 4, pp. 17–26. English translation in *Soviet Studies in Philosophy*, vol. 29, no. 2.

——— (1989b). "On Thoughts from Forbidden Zones." *Vestnik Moskovskogo universiteta*, ser. 12, *Teoriia nauchnogo kommunizma*, no. 3, pp. 42–52.

——— (1989c). "The Real Drama of Soviet History." *Nauka i zhizn'*, no. 12, pp. 37–45.

———— (1989d). "What Kind of Socialism?" *Pravda*, August 8.

Buzgalin, A. (1989). "In Search of the Path to the 'Realm of Freedom.' " *Obshchestvennye nauki*, no. 5, pp. 30–40.

Buzgalin, A., and Kolganov, A. (1989). "Time to Get Down to Business." *Sotsialisticheskii trud*, no. 3, pp. 42–46.

Cherniak, V. (1988). "It Is Shameful to Earn Little." *Literaturnaia gazeta*, November 23.

Chichilimov, V. (1987). "The Further Democratization of Society." *Kommunist Moldavii*, no. 9, pp. 73–80.

Diligenskii, G. (1989). "Who Is Afraid of Democracy?" *New Times*, no. 38, pp. 26–29.

Dzarasov, S. (1990). "Democratic Socialism: Economic Essence and Prospects." *Voprosy ekonomiki*, no. 2, pp. 39–51. English translation in *Problems of Economics*, vol. 33, no. 7.

Ekonomicheskaia gazeta (1988). "Recommendations." No. 9.

Ershova, S. (1988). "Elections and Choice." *Sovetskaia Estoniia*, September 15.

Fedoseev, P.N. (1989). "Ideological Unity of the Party and Socialist Pluralism of Opinions." *Sotsiologicheskie issledovaniia*, no. 5, pp. 13–22.

Gerchikov, V.I. (1989). "The Human Factor and Industrial Democracy." *Izvestiia sibirskogo otdeleniia Akademii nauk SSSR, Seriia ekonomiki i prikladnoi sotsiologii*, no. 1, pp. 32–42. English translation in *Soviet Sociology*, vol. 29, no. 2.

Gerchikov, V.I., and Proshkin, B.G. (1988). "Elections of Executives: Initial Experiences and Problems." *EKO*, no. 5, pp. 89–102. English translation in *Soviet Sociology*, vol. 28, no. 4.

Gordon, L.A., and Klopov, E. (1987). "The Main Strength of Revolutionary Transformations." *Kommunist*, no. 16, pp. 18–27.

Gordon, L.A.; Klopov, E.; and Petrov, T. (1987). "New Technical Reconstruction: Current Problems in the Light of Historical Experience." *Politicheskoe samoobrazovanie*, no. 2, pp. 3–12.

Gordon, L.A.; Monusova, G.A.; and Nazimova, A.K. (1987). "New Forms of Brigade Organization of Work: Problems, Contradictions, and Prospects." *Rabochii klass i sovremennyi mir*, no. 1, pp. 116–28.

Gordon, L.A., and Nazimova, A.K. (1983). "The Socio-Occupational Structure of Contemporary Soviet Society." *Rabochii klass i sovremennyi mir*, no. 2 (1983a), pp. 61–73, and no. 3 (1983b), pp. 59–72. English translation in *Soviet Sociology*, vol. 24, no. 1; reprinted in Yanowitch, 1986, pp. 3–61.

———— (1984). "Technical-Technological Progress and the Social Development of the Soviet Working Class." *Voprosy filosofii*, no. 7, pp. 18–38.

———— (1985). *Rabochii klass SSSR*. Moscow: Nauka.

———— (1986). "Shovel, Machine Tool, Control Panel." *Znanie—sila*, no. 2, pp. 11–14.

Gregory, P.R., and Stuart, R.C. (1986). *Soviet Economic Structure and Performance*, 3d ed. New York: Harper and Row.

Grushin, B.A. (1988). "Public Opinion in the System of Management."

Sotsiologicheskie issledovaniia, no. 3, pp. 24–29. English translation in *Soviet Sociology*, vol. 28, no. 4.

———— (1989). "Briefly about an Important Matter." *Informatsionnyi biulleten', Vsesoiuznyi tsentr izucheniia obshchestvennogo mneniia*, February, pp. 2–5.

Hewett, Ed A. (1988). *Reforming the Soviet Economy.* Washington, DC: The Brookings Institution.

Hirschhorn, Larry. (1986). *Beyond Mechanization.* Cambridge, MA: MIT Press.

Iadov, V.A. (1989). "Interview: The Voice of the People." *Pravda*, June 26. English translation in *Soviet Sociology*, vol. 29, no. 3.

Iakimenko, V. (1989). "Elements of Industrial Democracy." *Sotsialisticheskii trud*, no. 8, pp. 53–56.

Iarkho, A. (1988). "Legal Questions of Elections of Managers." *Sotsialisticheskii trud*, no. 10, pp. 64–69.

Il'inskii, I.P. (1987). *Sotsialisticheskoe samoupravlenie naroda.* Moscow: Mysl'.

Ionin, L. (1990). "A Society of Citizens." *Novoe vremia*, no. 2, p. 35.

Ivanov, V.N. (1987). *Trudovoi kollektiv: Pervichnaia iacheika sotsialisticheskogo samoupravleniia.* Moscow: Mysl'.

Kapeliush, Ia.S. (1989). "Public Opinion on Elections of Economic Managers." *Informatsionnyi biulleten', Vsesoiuznyi tsentr izucheniia obshchestvennogo mneniia*, January, pp. 10–27.

Katul'skii, E., and Kobiakov, A. (1988). "The Composition and Role of the Council of the Work Collective." *Sotsialisticheskii trud*, no. 5, pp. 67–69.

Kerimov, D.A., ed. (1976). *Sovetskaia demokratiia v period razvitogo sotsializma.* Moscow: Mysl'.

Khallik, K. (1987). "The Human Factor, Restructuring, and Responsibility." *Kommunist Estonii*, no. 2, pp. 18–22.

Kirichenko, N., and Shmarov, A. (1988). "Who Gains from Low Prices? Polemical Reflections." *Nedelia*, no. 30, p. 3.

Kliamkin, I. (1989). "Once Again on the Sources of Stalinism." *Politicheskoe obrazovanie*, no. 9, pp. 41–50.

Kliamkin, I., and Migranian, A. (1989). "Is an 'Iron Hand' Needed?" *Literaturnaia gazeta*, August 16.

Kolakowski, L. (1977). "Marxist Roots of Stalinism." In R.S. Tucker, ed., *Stalinism: Essays in Historical Interpretation*, pp. 283–98. New York: W.W. Norton.

Kolodii, A.F. (1989). "A Contribution to the Discussion on the Doctrinal Preconditions of the Deformation of Socialism." *Filosofskie nauki*, no. 12, pp. 61–68. English translation in *Soviet Studies in Philosophy*, vol. 29, no. 3.

Komilev, G. (1989). "Is It Easy to Elect the Director?" *Sovetskaia Estoniia*, March 1.

Kon, I. (1980). "Interview: To Be a Creator." *Literaturnaia gazeta*, December 26.

———— (1984a). "The Right to Creativity." *Pravda*, January 16.

——— (1984b). "Initiative and Control." *Novyi mir*, no. 6, pp. 264–65.

——— (1984c). *V poiskakh sebia*. Moscow: Izdatel'stvo politicheskoi literatury.

——— (1985). "The Psychology of Responsibility." *Znanie—sila*, no. 7, pp. 42–44.

Konstantinov, V. (1987). "Secret Voting." *Trud*, November 21.

Korshunova, V., and Novosel'tsev, M. (1989). *Sotsialisticheskii trud*, no. 3, pp. 68–73.

Kozlov, E. (1987). "Candidates: One's Own and Others." *Ekonomicheskaia gazeta*, no. 43.

Krasnov, M. (1988a). "The Work Collective: Democracy and Responsibility." *Politicheskoe obrazovanie*, no. 5, pp. 54–65.

——— (1988b). "Democracy, Law, and Production." *Politicheskoe obrazovanie*, no. 12, pp. 108–12.

Kudiukin, P.M. (1988). "Self-Management in Production: Experience, Theory, and Prospects." *Obshchestvennye nauki v SSSR. Problemy nauchnogo kommunizma*, ser. 1, no. 4, pp. 38–50.

Kurashvili, B. (1988a). "Racing to Democracy." *Moscow News*, no. 9.

——— (1988b). "Sovereign Power: From the Past to the Future." *Izvestiia*, November 15.

——— (1989a). "The Formula of Socialism." *Kommunist Estonii*, no. 5, pp. 12–23.

——— (1989b). "Models of Socialism." *Sovetskoe gosudarstvo i pravo*, no. 8, pp. 99–110. English translation in *Soviet Sociology*, vol. 29, no. 4.

Lachinov, Iu.N. (1988). "Economic Functions of the Family." *EKO*, no. 7, pp. 19–29.

Lapin, N.I., ed. (1980). *Sotsial'nye faktory novovvedenii v organizationnykh sistemakh*. Moscow: Vsesoiuznyi nauchno-issledovatel'nyi institut sistemnykh issledovanii.

———, ed. (1981). *Struktura innovatsionnogo protsessa*. Moscow: Vsesoiuznyi nauchno-issledovatel'nyi institut sistemnykh issledovanii.

———, ed. (1982). *Innovatsionnye protsessy*. Moscow: Vsesoiuznyi nauchno-issledovatel'nyi institut sistemnykh issledovanii.

Lapin, N.I., and Prigozhin, A.I. (1982). "Social Innovations: A New Direction in Organizational Psychology in the West." *Psikhologicheskii zhurnal*, no. 5, pp. 159–65.

Lapin, N.I., and Sazonov, B.V. (1985). "The Human Factor in Innovations." *Psikhologicheskii zhurnal*, no. 4, pp. 64–72.

Law on the State Enterprise (Association) (1987). English translation in *Current Digest of the Soviet Press*, vol. 39, no. 30 (1987); see also *Soviet Statutes and Decisions*, vol. 26, no. 4.

Leont'eva, E. (1989). "Social Conflict." *Voprosy ekonomiki*, no. 4, pp. 120–29. English translation in *Problems of Economics*, vol. 32, no. 8.

Lisichkin, G. (1986). "Charity from Someone Else's Pocket." *Literaturnaia gazeta*, February 19.

——— (1987). "The Yearning for Equality." *Literaturnaia gazeta*, June 24.

————— (1988). "People and Things." *Druzhba narodov*, no. 1, pp. 207–39.

Literaturnaia gazeta (1987). "How the First Secretary of the Moscow Writers' Organization Was Elected." October 21.

Liubimov, L. (1989). "To What System Does the USA Belong?" *Literaturnaia gazeta*, June 28.

Loshak, V. (1989). "The Fourth Director." *Moscow News*, no. 1.

Markov, V. (1985). "Distribution According to Work, and Balancing Incomes and Commodity Resources." *Sotsialisticheskii trud*, no. 4, pp. 46–56.

Maslennikov, V.A. (1987). "Discussing the Draft of the Law of the USSR on the State Enterprise (Association)." *Sovetskoe gosudarstvo i pravo*, no. 5, pp. 54–56.

Merkurov, G. (1988). "Mechanisms of Power and Democracy." *Politicheskoe obrazovanie*, no. 16, pp. 59–62.

Merzlikina, M. (1989). "Determining Authority." *Sotsialisticheskii trud*, no. 5, pp. 57–61.

Migranian, A.M. (1987). "Interrelations of the Individual, Society, and the State in the Political Theory of Marxism (The Problem of the Democratization of Socialist Society)." *Voprosy filosofii*, no. 8, pp. 75–91. English translation in *Soviet Studies in Philosophy*, vol. 27, no. 3.

————— (1988a). "Society and State." *Znanie—sila*, no. 12, pp. 1–7.

————— (1988b). "The Braking Mechanism in the Political System and the Means of Overcoming It." In Iu.N. Afanas'ev, ed., *Inogo ne dano*, pp. 97–121. Moscow: Progress.

————— (1989a). "The Long Road to a European Home." *Novyi mir*, no. 7, pp. 166–84. English translation in *Soviet Law and Government*, vol. 29, no. 3; abridged translation in *Current Digest of the Soviet Press*, vol. 41, no. 42 (1989), p. 8.

————— (1989b). "Reform of the Political System: The View of a Political Scientist." *Filosofskie nauki*, no. 9, pp. 17–25.

Mikul'skii, K. (1988). "Differentiation of Labor Incomes under Socialism: Essence, Functions, Criteria, Parameters." *Voprosy ekonomiki*, no. 8, pp. 3–16.

Morozov, V. (1988). "Elections of Economic Executives: A Genuinely Democratic Character." *Partiinaia zhizn'*, no. 16, pp. 56–59.

Morozov, V., and Sorokin, N. (1987). "To Whom Should the Collective Be Entrusted?" *Ekonomicheskaia gazeta*, no. 23.

Moses, J. (1987). "Worker Self-Management and the Reformist Alternatives in Soviet Labour Policy, 1979–1985." *Soviet Studies*, no. 2, pp. 205–28.

Muzdybaev, K. (1983). *Psikhologiia otvetstvennosti*. Leningrad: Nauka.

Nazimova, A.K., and Gordon, L.A. (1986). "Scientific and Technical Progress and the Production Activity of the Working Class." *Rabochii klass i sovremennyi mir*, no. 4, pp. 49–58. English translation in *Soviet Sociology*, vol. 26, no. 2.

Nikiforov, A. (1990). "Will Marxism Survive Restructuring?" *Obshchestvennye nauki*, no. 3, pp. 115–28.

Orlov, B.S. (1988). "*Perestroika* and the Theoretical Approach of Social Democracy." *Rabochii klass i sovremennyi mir*, no. 5, pp. 125–31.

———— (1989). "Social Democracy: A Portrait without Black Retouching." *Kommunist Estonii*, no. 11, pp. 53–71.

———— (1990a). "Free Rostrum." *Ogonek*, no. 36, pp. 18–19.

———— (1990b). "Should Social Democratization Be Feared?" *Novoe vremia*, no. 6, pp. 24–25.

Peregudov, S. (1990). "The Social-Democratic Model of Social Relations." *Mirovaia ekonomika i mezhdunarodnye otnosheniia*, no. 5, pp. 5–20.

Perlamutrov, V. (1989). "To Live on What One Has Earned." *Kommunist Belorussii*, no. 8, pp. 35–43.

Petrik, A. (1987). "The Collective Selects the Executive." *Politicheskoe obrazovanie*, no. 11, pp. 57–65.

Piiasheva, L. (1989). "A Look at the Social Democrats' Experience." *International Affairs*, May, pp. 94–99, 136.

———— (1990). "What Can We Expect from 'People's Socialism'?" *Dialog*, no. 9, pp. 72–79.

Pinsker, B. (1989). "The Bureaucratic Chimera." *Znamia*, no. 11, pp. 183–202.

Popov, G. (1989). "On the Benefit of Inequality." *Literaturnaia gazeta*, October 4, p. 10.

———— (1990a). "To Our Readers." *Voprosy ekonomiki*, no. 1, pp. 3–13. English translation in *Problems of Economics*, vol. 33, no. 6.

———— (1990b). "Dangers of Democracy." *The New York Review of Books*, August 16.

Postal'nyi, V. (1987). "Democracy: A Powerful Impulse." *Ekonomicheskaia gazeta*, no. 13.

Prigozhin, A.I. (1983). *Organizatsii: Sistemy i liudi*. Moscow: Izdatel'stvo politicheskoi literatury. English translation of chapter 6 in Yanowitch, 1989.

———— (1984). "Managerial Innovations and Economic Experiments." *Kommunist*, no. 7, pp. 57–67. English translation in *Problems of Economics*, vol. 26, no. 10.

———— (1985). "The Potential of an Experiment." *Kommunist*, no. 5, pp. 30–40.

Puginskii, B.I. (1989). "The Rights of Enterprises: Law and Practice." *Sovetskoe gosudarstvo i pravo*, no. 8, pp. 28–35.

Rabochii klass i sovremennyi mir (1987). Editorial. "Urgent Changes." No. 2, pp. 3–9.

Radaev, V. (1988). "Emancipating Initiative." *Ekonomicheskaia gazeta*, no. 47.

Rakitskaia, G.Ia. (1986). "The Socioeconomic Nature of Scientific and Technical Progress." *Ekonomicheskie nauki*, no. 12, pp. 37–45. English translation in *Problems of Economics*, vol. 30, no. 6.

———— (1989). "Socialist Democracy: Politico-Economic Aspects." *Voprosy ekonomiki*, no. 7, pp. 35–47. English translation in *Problems of Economics*, vol. 31, no. 10.

Rakitskaia, G.Ia., and Rakitskii, B.V. (1988). "Reflections on Restructuring as a Social Revolution." *EKO*, no. 5, pp. 3–28. English translation in *Soviet Sociology*, vol. 28, no. 5.

Rakitskii, B.V. (1987). "The Reform of Management and the Dialectics of Interests." *Ekonomicheskaia gazeta*, no. 43 (October), p. 15. English translation in *Soviet Sociology*, vol. 27, no. 3; reprinted in Yanowitch, 1989.

Rimashevskaia, N.M. (1988). "Public Well-Being: Myth and Reality." *EKO*, no. 7, pp. 3–195. English translation in *Problems of Economics*, vol. 31, no. 12.

——— (1989). "Justice or Equality?" In A.G. Vishnevskii, ed., *V chelovecheskom izmerenii*, pp. 364–77. Moscow: Progress.

Riurikov, Iu.B. (1986). "An Upheaval in Civilization (Some Barriers on the Path to Communism and the Role of Man)." *Voprosy ekonomiki*, no. 9, pp. 133–43.

Rogovin, V.Z. (1982). "Distributive Relations as a Factor Intensifying Production." *Sotsiologicheskie issledovaniia*, no. 1, pp. 7–18.

——— (1985a). "Social Justice and Some Questions of Improving Distributive Relations." *Politicheskoe samoobrazovanie*, no. 6, pp. 44–52. English translation in *Soviet Law and Government*, vol. 25, no. 1.

——— (1985b). "Personal Property." *Komsomol'skaia pravda*, November 12.

——— (1986). "Social Justice and the Distribution of Vital Goods." *Voprosy filosofii*, no. 9, pp. 3–20. English translation in *Soviet Sociology*, vol. 26, no. 3; reprinted in Yanowitch, 1989.

——— (1989). "From Stalinist Equality to Brezhnev's Openness of Incomes." *EKO*, no. 9, pp. 134–45.

Roundtable (1987). *Trud*, November 24.

——— (1988a). "Is Economic Reform Possible without Restructuring in Politics?" *Voprosy ekonomiki*, no. 6, pp. 3–22. English translation in *Problems of Economics*, vol. 31, no. 10.

——— (1988b). "Western Democracy and Problems of Current Social Development." *Mirovaia ekonomika i mezhdunarodnye otnosheniia*, no. 11, pp. 5–18. English translation in *Problems of Economics*, vol. 32, no. 2.

——— (1988c). "Socialist Pluralism." *Sotsiologicheskie issledovaniia*, no. 5, pp. 6–24. English translation in *Soviet Sociology*, vol. 28, no. 6.

——— (1989a), "Western Democracy and Problems of Current Social Development." *Mirovaia ekonomika i mezhdunarodnye otnosheniia*, no. 1, pp. 71–84.

——— (1989b). "Strikes in the USSR: A New Social Reality." *Sotsiologicheskie issledovaniia*, no. 1, pp. 21–36. English translation in *Soviet Sociology*, vol. 29, no. 2.

——— (1989c). "Pluralism in Socialist Society: The Means of Affirming It under Conditions of *Perestroika*." *Vestnik Moskovskogo universiteta*, ser. 12, *Teoriia nauchnogo kommunizma*, no. 4, pp. 3–72.

Ryvkina, R. (1987). "Overcoming the Braking Mechanism." *Sovetskaia Estoniia*, November 11. English translation in *Soviet Sociology*, vol. 27, no. 2.

Seliunin, V. (1989). "Planned Anarchy or a Balance of Interests?" *Znamia*, no. 11, pp. 203–20.

Sergeev, A. (1989). "From Today to Tomorrow, or to the Day before Yesterday?" *Ekonomicheskie nauki*, no. 9, pp. 121–31.

Sheinis, V. (1988a). "Capitalism, Socialism, and the Economic Mechanism of Modern Production." *Mirovaia ekonomika i mezhdunarodnye otnosheniia*, no. 9, pp. 5–23.

——— (1988b). "In Search of Optimal Paths of Restructuring." *Vestnik Moskovskogo universiteta*, ser. 12, *Teoriia nauchnogo kommunizma*, no. 6, pp. 13–27.

Shkurko, S. (1989). "The Mechanism of Self-Management." *Sotsialisticheskii trud*, no. 8, pp. 49–53.

Shkurko, S., and Meshcherkin, A. (1987). "The Experiment and After." *Sotsialisticheskii trud*, no. 6, pp. 97–105.

Shokhin, A.N. (1989). *Sotsial'nye problemy perestroiki*. Moscow: Ekonomika.

Shokhin, A.N.; Guzanova, N.; and Liberman, L. (1988). "Prices through the Eyes of the Population." *Literaturnaia gazeta*, September 14. English translation in *Problems of Economics*, vol. 32, no. 2.

Shpil'ko, S. (1989). "That 'Terrible' Private Property." *Nedelia*, no. 52.

Shustov, A. (1988). "A Sad Unanimity." *Literaturnaia gazeta*, August 24.

Strashun, B. (1987). "Democratization: The Motor of Restructuring." *Politicheskoe obrazovanie*, no. 11, pp. 48–56.

Sungorkin, N. (1987). "How the Director Was Elected." *Sotsialisticheskii trud*, no. 5, pp. 81–85.

Tikhomirov, Iu.A. (1988). *Demokratiia i ekonomika*. Moscow: Sovetskaia Rossiia.

Torkanovskii, E. (1987). "Socialist Self-Management of Production." *Voprosy ekonomiki*, no. 8, pp. 46–55. English translation in *Problems of Economics*, vol. 30, no. 10; reprinted in Yanowitch, 1989.

——— (1988a). "Democracy for the Director." *Moskovskie novosti*, no. 21.

——— (1988b). "What Lies ahead for Self-Management in Production?" *Kommunist*, no. 12, pp. 48–56. English translation in *Problems of Economics*, vol. 31, no. 12.

——— (1990). "Property and Self-Management of the Work Collective." *Voprosy ekonomiki*, no. 9, pp. 103–11.

Tsipko, A. (1988–1989). "Sources of Stalinism." *Nauka i zhizn'*, no. 11 (1988a), pp. 45–55; no. 12 (1988b), pp. 40–47; no. 1 (1989a), pp. 46–56; no. 2 (1989b), pp. 53–61. English translation in *Soviet Law and Government*, vol. 29, nos. 1, 2.

——— (1990a). "Contradictions in the Teachings of Karl Marx." *Vestnik Moskovskogo universiteta*, ser. 12, *Sotsial'no-politicheskie issledovaniia*, no. 2, pp. 77–83.

——— (1990b). "Do We Have Good Principles?" *Novyi mir*, no. 4, pp. 173–204.

Tucker, R.C., ed. (1978). *The Marx-Engels Reader*, 2d ed. New York: W.W. Norton.

Valiuzhenich, G. (1990). "The Secrecy of Deposits." *Argumenty i fakty*, no. 13.

Vashchenko, V. (1988). "Elections—For the Work at Hand." *EKO*, no. 11, pp. 54–58.

Vasil'ev, V.A. (1989). "Pluralism and Dialectical Materialist Monism." *Filosofskie nauki*, no. 11, pp. 98–101.

Vaziulin, V.A. (1988). "In Search of Optimal Paths of Restructuring." *Vestnik Moskovskogo universiteta*, ser. 12, *Teoriia nauchnogo kommunizma*, no. 6, pp. 27–28.

Veber, A.B. (1988). "Industrial Democracy and the Efficiency of Production." *Rabochii klass i sovremennyi mir*, no. 5, pp. 52–63.

Vedomosti Verkhovnogo soveta Soiuza Sovetskikh Sotsialisticheskikh Respublik (1983). No. 25 (2203), June 22.

Vilchek, V. (1989). "Right, Left, Which Side?" *Literaturnaia gazeta*, October 18.

Vodovozov, N., and Novikov, V. (1988). "Choice." *Moscow News*, no. 34.

Volkonskii, V. (1990). "The 'Cultured Huckster' among Us." *Kommunist*, no. 1, pp. 58–64. English translation in *Problems of Economics*, vol. 33, no. 4.

Yanowitch, M. (1978). "Pressures for More Participatory Forms of Economic Organization in the Soviet Union." *Economic Analysis and Workers' Management*, nos. 3–4, pp. 403–17.

——— (1985). *Work in the Soviet Union: Attitudes and Issues.* Armonk, NY: M.E. Sharpe.

———, ed. (1986). *The Social Structure of the USSR: Recent Soviet Studies.* Armonk, NY: M.E. Sharpe.

———, ed. (1989). *New Directions in Soviet Social Thought: An Anthology.* Armonk, NY: M.E. Sharpe.

Zaslavskaia, T.I. (1986). "Creative Activity of the Masses: Social Reserves of Growth." *EKO*, no. 3, pp. 3–25. English translation in *Problems of Economics*, vol. 29, no. 11; reprinted in Zaslavskaia, 1989a.

——— (1989a). *A Voice of Reform: Essays by Tat'iana I. Zaslavskaia.* Ed. Murray Yanowitch. Armonk, NY: M.E. Sharpe.

——— (1989b). "The Economy in the Mirror of Public Opinion." *Voprosy ekonomiki*, no. 11, pp. 127–28. English translation in *Soviet Sociology*, vol. 29, no. 5.

——— (1989c). "Interview: To Live with Open Eyes." *Kommunist*, no. 8, pp. 45–54. English translation in *Soviet Sociology*, vol. 29, no. 3.

Zaslavskaia, T.I., and Kupriianova, Z.V., eds. (1987). *Sotsial'no-ekonomicheskoe razvitie sibirskogo sela.* Novosibirsk: Nauka.

Zdravomyslov, A.G. (1987). "New Sociopolitical Thinking and the Problem of the Technological Challenge." *Rabochii klass i sovremennyi mir*, no. 6, pp. 3–15. English translation in *Soviet Sociology*, vol. 27, no. 3; reprinted in Yanowitch, 1989.

Zhezhko, I.V. (1982). "The Social Consequences of the Scientific and Technical Revolution and Problems of Managerial Innovations." *Voprosy filosofii*, no. 6, pp. 150–53.

Zolotov, A. (1987). "The Participation of Working People in the Management of Socialist Production: The Political-Economic Aspect." *Ekonomicheskie nauki*, no. 5, pp. 126–31.

INDEX

Murray Yanowitch is professor emeritus of economics at Hofstra University in Hempstead, New York. He is the author of numerous works about Soviet social, economic, and labor issues including *Social and Economic Inequality in the Soviet Union: Six Studies* and *Work in the Soviet Union: Attitudes and Issues*. He edited the volumes *Social Stratification and Mobility in the USSR, Soviet Work Attitudes: The Issue of Participation in Management, The Social Structure of the USSR: Recent Soviet Studies, A Voice of Reform: Essays by Tat'iana I. Zaslavskaia*, and *New Directions in Soviet Social Thought: An Anthology*. He is also the editor of the translation journals *Soviet Sociology* and *Problems of Economics*.

For Product Safety Concerns and Information please contact our EU
representative GPSR@taylorandfrancis.com
Taylor & Francis Verlag GmbH, Kaufingerstraße 24, 80331 München, Germany